Timeless Vows
Five Tales of Love

Ruth A. Casie
Lita Harris
Emma Kaye
Nicole S. Patrick
Julie Rowe

Timeless Scribes
Publishing

Timeless Scribes Publishing LLC

Print   ISBN-10: 0986246417
         ISBN-13: 978-0-9862464-1-8

Digital ISBN-10: 0986246409
         ISBN-13: 978-0-9862464-0-1

Cover created by Alchemy Book Covers and Design
Edited by Mallory Braus
Copy Edited by Michael Mandarano

This is a work of fiction. Names, characters, places and incidents are
either the product of the author's imagination or are used fictitiously,
and any resemblance to actual persons, living or dead, business
establishments, events or locales is entirely coincidental.

This edition published by arrangement with Timeless Scribes
Publishing LLC.

www.TimelessScribes.com

Contents

Introduction

by Jennifer Probst

http://www.jenniferprobst.com

NYT Bestselling Author of the *Marriage to a Billionaire Series*

With the onset of Spring popping all around us, May is a special month to celebrate some of the greatest emotional events such as graduations, proms, and of course, weddings.

There is something about a wedding that brings a wistful sigh or wraps us up in a past memory of romance. The stunning bride in white, the sweet scent of roses, the line of colorful dresses, the long walk down an aisle toward a new future while poignant music caresses our ears.

In this special collection of five stories, *Timeless Vows* centers around a weekend wedding that changes each couple forever. We are swept to the remote mountains of Maine at The Loon Lake Inn to rediscover passion, love, forgiveness, and to be healed. Each couple faces their own barriers to love—from the struggles of learning about real commitment and communication, to a heartfelt trip back in time to see if love can once again be rediscovered after a tragedy. Enjoy the thrill of a first college crush returning with the promise of more, and the fight to keep a marriage alive amidst the daily challenges of life, to the journey of forgiveness and second chances.

These stories will remind readers that each relationship is unique, full of ups and downs, and heartbreakingly fragile yet fiercely strong in its beauty. You're invited to step into The Loon Lake Inn and witness a wedding...and meet five couples who will find their own happy-ever-after amidst the most timeless journey of all: love.

Forsaking All Others

Ruth A. Casie

♥♥♥

Morgan and Margot are wild about each other. But early on in their relationship, Morgan was focused on establishing himself with one of New York's most prestigious law firms and Margot was busy making a name for herself in the antiques business. For the past ten years commitment was not something either of them wanted.

A visit to Morgan's brother and sister-in-law changes both their lives. Now it seems all the two of them can think of is making a commitment—they just don't know how to tell each other. They are both afraid of driving the other away.

Morgan keeps reminding Margot she doesn't want a commitment, hoping she's changed her mind. Margot thinks Morgan needs to see someone else interested in her to force him into action.

In truth, all they need to do is talk to each other and say what's in their hearts. Will they come to their senses or deny the loving relationship they both desire?

♥♥♥

Dedicated to ~

Jen, Lita, Nicole, Julie, and Desi. You make the hard writing easier, the puns funnier, and chocolate (and wine) tastes better when we're together.

Olivia and Alex. I love you more than you will ever know.

Mallory Braus, for making me work hard and keep reaching for the stars.

Paul. You are my beloved and my beloved is mine. With all my love that's always yours.

Forsaking All Others
by Ruth A. Casie

She didn't mean to intrude. All she'd wanted was to step out on the wide porch for a breath of cool air to stop her head from spinning. Now she couldn't leave fast enough. What was she doing here straddling the threshold, pinned to the spot like a fly in amber, a death grip on the French door handles? Leave. Give them a little privacy—but she couldn't move. Instead she watched Gabe embrace her close friend Viv. His fingertips whispered down her back while his other hand drifted down her side and rested on her hip. But it was the smoldering looks they had for each other that made her breath catch.

It was hard to imagine Viv getting married. They'd known each other for years. She was five years older and would always think of Viv as a flighty kid. But it was easy to see Gabe and Viv's commitment to each other. Commitment. She blew out the word in exasperation. She hadn't understood how much she'd wanted that from

Morgan—until now.

A burst of loud music behind her broke the spell. She stepped back into the banquet room and closed the doors without making a sound. In all the years she'd known Gabe and Viv she'd never seen them so love struck. Their bed was a playground, but they were die-hard singles—at least that was what Viv had told her. Sure they lived together, but…well, it was convenient. They were good friends with benefits, that's what they were. What a joke. She turned and glimpsed the bride and groom through the glass doors. How did she not see they were head over heels in love?

With her back to the door, she scanned the crowded bachelor/bachelorette party to see if Morgan had returned. He'd stepped out an hour ago. Business, he'd said. *Aren't you glad we're not doing this?* She thought about his words from earlier in the day. No, damn it. This is what she wanted. *Do you hear me, Morgan Stuart? I. Want. Forever.*

The DJ had almost everyone—including every woman present—doing a line dance on the packed dance floor. She had a clear view of the bar where the men were hanging out, gawking and making comments while they had their drinks. Nope, he wasn't there, either. She was about to give up when a movement by the nest of cocktail tables captured her attention.

Morgan raised his bottle of beer in salute. "And I only want forever with you," she murmured. She ran her hands down her snug black dress—making sure it clung in all the right places—then maneuvered across the crowded room, eager to get to him. She wanted to see if his eyes smoldered when he looked at her. As soon as she reached him she realized she needed more courage. She removed the bottle from his hand and took a swallow.

"Whoa. You don't like beer. Remember?" Ignoring

his outstretched hand, she took another gulp and tried not to screw up her face. The stuff was vile, but she wasn't going to give him the satisfaction.

Those little pink things—the ones with vodka, vermouth and strawberries that she'd had all afternoon—slid down so easily, along with the shots she'd had a few minutes ago with the girls in the bridal party. At the moment she didn't care what she drank. Something wet and mind numbing was what she wanted.

Maybe the beer would steady the room and stop it from spinning. No, the dancers were a blur and now her stomach was complaining.

Since the beer made her stomach queasier, she placed her hands on the back of the chair and held on for dear life. A sideways glimpse was all she needed to see Morgan shaking his head.

"You're going to regret this in the morning," he said, bending close to her. She closed her eyes and tried to control a shudder as his low voice and warm breath bathed her ear. She turned to face him, his lips a kiss away and his eyes…his eyes—

"You two are next. You know why?" They glanced at Dave, a groomsman, who stood beside them looking at the mob on the dance floor. "Because you're the last holdouts. How long have you been together? Ten years? When are you going to tie the knot?"

The bottle dangled from her hand. Morgan retrieved his beer and exchanged it for a large glass of water. One sip then she chugged it all.

"We're happy the way we are. You can ask Margot. She'd be the first to tell you she doesn't need a piece of paper." Why didn't he just take a knife to her heart? This wasn't the first time he put it into words. She didn't want commitment eight years ago, but now…

"Why spoil a good thing?" she said in a matter-of-fact tone and gave Dave her most dazzling smile. What else could she say? It was obvious Morgan liked the arrangement. She got on her tiptoes and kissed Morgan's lips. She searched his eyes, trying to see if that special look, the one Gabe had for his Viv, was there. But with Dave next to them, Morgan had his game face on. When it suited him he could be hard to read. He was one of the best corporate attorneys in New York. This evening he was the poker-face master.

She choked down regrets that they weren't alone. A family. The idea had been on her mind since their trip to Star Island. Now, at the wedding, she knew she wanted one of her own and she wanted one with Morgan. She'd loved him from the start but right now, at this moment, she understood how much. She loved his sense of humor, his unconditional acceptance, his steadfast friendship, his closeness to his family, his Chris Pine blue eyes, his voice, his touch, his…everything.

The doors opened with a burst of air when Viv and Gabe came in laughing. The sudden dip in temperature sent a chill up her back that made her shudder. Morgan snaked a protective arm around her. "You okay?"

She melted into his side and nodded while she inhaled the woodsy scent of his cologne. It was a special fragrance she'd had made for him five birthdays ago. Now he bought it by the gallon and kept a small bottle on his well-organized bathroom shelf. Well organized, compared to hers, that is. His area was neat and orderly. Her shelf—that was another story. She was more the creative clutter type.

For Morgan, everything in his life had a place—everything. And her place was "no commitment." It was something he'd been telling her over the past few months. Did he know she wanted more?

Or was he warning her off, telling her not to ask

because she wouldn't like the answer? She might have had an idea that he was interested in someone else but she knew he wasn't. None of the signs were there. He was as engaged with her and their friends as he had ever been. He was attentive and thoughtful. Oh, they had their disagreements and arguments, but they settled their differences before they went to sleep. No, things were going well with their relationship, but they weren't moving forward. What would it take?

He put the empty bottle on the table, handed her purse to her and moved them toward the door. She glanced around. The crowded room had thinned while the DJ packed up. Her head rang at the sound of clanking glasses as the staff cleaned up and got the tables ready for the morning crowd. "Where're we going?"

"I don't know about you, but I'm exhausted. I'm going to sleep." They continued on to the grand lobby. Now that her liquid courage had kicked in, she'd speak to him tonight and tell him she wanted a commitment, wanted to get married, or else. Or else what? She tripped over something on the floor; Morgan held on to her.

"Easy. Are you okay?" She didn't know if she was or not.

"Sure," she said with a wave of her hand. What if he didn't want to marry her? She glanced at his strong profile. What if he walked away? No, she didn't want to lose him. She loved him. No, no, this arrangement was fine, she tried to convince herself. She bit back the building tears, swallowed around the hot knot in her throat and moved toward the lobby. Things were fine the way they were. She forced herself to think of other, more pleasant things.

The Loon Lake Inn was a picturesque log cabin with two wings of guest rooms joined at the large central area. She took a deep breath to steady her spinning head and caught the scent of flowers scattered around everywhere. They passed the comfortable overstuffed chairs that created intimate conversations areas. The focal point of the room was the large fieldstone fireplace. She could imagine how cozy it would be in the winter, cuddling with Morgan by the fire with a mulled wine or hot toddy. Today, the hearth was cold and filled with a large basket of roses. What had been fragrant two minutes ago had become overwhelming and cloying. Her stomach growled—or was it those pink things she drank that were threatening to erupt? Or was it the possibility of losing Morgan? She hurried and moved on.

She fixed her gaze on the long flight of stairs and knew she wouldn't make it to the top. She opted for the elevator. "Why would they need an elevator for a building with two floors?" She didn't know but she could kiss the innkeepers.

"Handicap access would be my guess," Morgan said as he held the elevator door for her. She nodded and buried her face in Morgan's chest for the short ride. The glass capsule ran up the outside of the building and the notion of watching the landscape glide by was more than her stomach could take.

"Our floor, m'lady." He kissed her forehead, draped his arm around her and led her down the hall. By the time they reached their door she noted that her knight was armed with the key. In addition to being gallant and dashing, the man was efficient.

Refusing to play the role of the damsel in distress, she plucked the key out of his hand and tried to insert it into the lock. On the fourth attempt, he put his hand over hers and helped guide her to the target. She turned the key and with a loud click that exploded like the report of a shotgun, Morgan turned the knob. The door opened and they stepped in.

The room was spacious and comfortable. The pale yellow walls and crisp white trim were soothing. The splashes of blue, orange and green floral chintz on the sofa and club chairs made the room homey.

Her heart pounded but she wasn't sure if it was from her liquid courage or the pouty, sexy expression on Morgan's face. She wiggled out of her black dress and draped it over the chair. Standing in her lacy underwear, she unhooked her bra, took off her panties and put them on top of her dress. Left in her strappy high heels, she took them off, too, and set them next to the chair. On her way to the bathroom she grabbed her nightshirt from her open suitcase and gave him a wet kiss on his lips. She kept her eyes closed.

"Did you hear? The band Gabe hired had to cancel," he called to her.

"What are they going to do? They're not hiring that awful DJ who played tonight?" She had trouble with the toothpaste. Every time she squeezed the tube it squirted into the sink. After the third try she shrugged and brushed her teeth sans paste.

"He wasn't so bad. But no, he's not available. Gabe needed help with—" She ran the water to wash up. "…Gabe and I spoke to…" She dried her face with the fluffy towel and didn't hear a word he said until she glided out of the bathroom. "Everything is all set. He asked me to go over the music with her."

How nice—the inn had turndown service. She inspected the sheets for the chocolate and when she didn't find it, shrugged. She scooted under the covers, leaving one leg hanging out over the edge, touching the floor. *Coward.* She'd talk to him tomorrow. She was asleep before her head hit the pillow.

♥♥♥

Morgan stared at her. He bit the side of his cheek in a Bruce Willis smirk that drove her crazy. Those high heels drove him wild. They made it look like her feet were bare, as bare as she was. His gaze ran up her body. She didn't have to stand naked in front of him for his body to react, although he had no problem with the view. It made him warm...all over. She'd be surprised if she was aware she was standing there naked. Exhibitionism wasn't her game. She had a quiet sexuality that screamed to him. He picked up her dress, along with her underclothes, and placed them on the chair, her original target.

He pulled the fancy pillows off the bed, stacked them with care at the side of the dresser and turned down the covers. As smashed as she was, he doubted she'd wait to get under them when she came to sleep.

He got undressed and leaned against the bathroom doorjamb wearing the bottoms of his pajamas, waiting for his turn. Perhaps it was her dedication to her business that got in the way of her making a commitment to him—no, to them. She'd been under pressure—working hard at her antiques business. Her latest project came together this weekend at the Boyles Auction House. It was a big deal on both the professional and personal levels. She'd come a long way over the past ten years. She networked with several rabid collectors who paid her well, not only for the items she sourced for them but for her opinion as well. When she had taken over her parents' little antiques shop, no one expected her to become a go-to person for high-quality pieces. He didn't doubt her ability for a minute and he didn't think the fact that he loved her clouded his view. Yeah, she was pretty special.

In general, she had self-control. The party girl was a

side of Margot he didn't see often. She earned the partying as well as the headache she'd have in the morning. Blowing off a little steam never hurt.

He'd make sure she'd be okay.

She stumbled past him, her makeup not quite off, wearing his pajama top. She pulled the sheets every which way, looking for something before she flopped on the bed faceup. Her left foot was planted on the ground.

Oh yeah, her headache was going to be a doozy.

He washed up and kept his eyes on her in the mirror. Satisfied she was all right, he sat in bed and scanned his business email on his cell phone. A message from George Hughes, an attorney he was friends with from England, sat in his inbox. He sent George a quick note to tell him the arrangements were completed as planned and wished him luck at tomorrow's auction. George's clients wanted to obtain original pieces that belonged to their centuries-old Fayne Manor estate. Morgan had introduced George to Margot. With the help of her father's contacts, she found a piece in excellent condition that was scheduled to go up for auction tomorrow at the prestigious Boyles Auction House in New York City.

There was a message from Eloise, his sister-in-law. She sent a new picture of baby Lily along with a note wishing him luck. He glanced at Margot, her long hair spread over the pillow, and he knew he was doing the right thing.

He hoped she agreed with him.

He turned off the light and slid between the sheets. He put his hands behind his head. His eyes focused on the blinking red dot on the ceiling smoke detector but his mind raced. He'd never fall asleep. He thought of all the things Gabe had asked him to handle for the weekend. Now, with the band canceling, Gabe had asked him for help with the contract. His pre-wedding list was expanding.

Alan, his brother, had expanded their technology company and opened an office on Star Island off the coast of St. Thomas. It was a great place for Alan and Eloise to raise Lily. He knew they'd both be great parents. When he and Margot visited them, he got a taste of family life and knew that's what he'd been working toward. When they were packing to leave, Alan had spoken to him. He'd decided he'd speak to Margot. Several times he tried to bring up the subject while they waited at the airport.

Airport. Gabe's list. How had his mind wandered onto Star Island and Margot? In the morning he needed to confirm the airport pickups with the driver. Margot's gentle snort distracted him. He checked to make sure she was all right. The crease on her brow had smoothed and her eyelids fluttered in her sleep. He hoped she dreamed of their time with Alan and Eloise and playing with Lily.

He was a lucky man.

She understood his dry sense of humor and knew how to cajole him out of his attorney mind-set. He hadn't expected their trip to Star Island to be such a revelation for him. She flew to the island and pitched right in when the baby's nurse had needed to cancel. He'd had no idea she knew what to do with a baby, but she was a natural. It was easy to see her as a mother even though neither of them had mentioned wanting a family.

Shit, he hadn't known he wanted a family until he watched her with little Lily. A father. He was hardworking and would be a great dad. Her father was hardworking and a well-established trial attorney who loved antiques second only to his wife and daughter. The antiques shop had been his hobby. Margot was his one employee. When her parents retired to the south of France, it was natural for Margot to take over the shop. It was a bargain.

He met Margot at the bargaining table. Her father

didn't want to turn the business over to her until she went over all the papers with an independent attorney. Morgan was a magnet for on-the-spot legal questions from friends and family. He'd grown used to it. Not that he liked it, but it came in small print on the bottom of his law school diploma. *Ad quaestionem respondendum religiose a familiae et amicis—gratis.* Mrs. Ball, his middle school Latin teacher, would cringe at that translation. Morgan had groaned when Gabe stopped him after their softball game and told him Viv's close friend needed legal counsel on a business deal. His list was filled—the list, goddamn it. *Stay on message, Morgan.* Five minutes, that's all he needed to get his thoughts organized.

Tomorrow, he'd get the band contract from Gabe and review the cancelation clause. He was sure he could get Viv and Gabe a better settlement. That would take a few hours. A few hours, that's how long it had taken for Margot to send over all her legal papers after she hired him. Two days later he met her, right before they sat with her dad. The agreement her father proposed was fair, but he'd argued a better one for her.

Over the next several months they met over dinner—sometimes pizza, other times the cheap French restaurant near her antiques shop—and hammered out the corporate papers and tax implications. Long after the last *t* was crossed and *i* dotted, they were still meeting for dinner.

She'd made it clear from the start she didn't want a commitment. Too busy with the business, she'd said. A relationship wasn't her priority. He was sure something else was behind it but gave her space.

He'd been right. One night, after softball, before he and Margot moved into their apartment together, Gabe had offered the information. The guy, Zack, must have been blind.

Well, Zack's loss was Morgan's gain.

Everything went along fine. They moved in together eight years ago. Neither of them had any complaints.

The flash of his cell phone display caught his attention. It was updating. He reached over and placed it facedown. Margot mumbled in her sleep and turned onto her side, nuzzling next to him. He moved the hair out of her eyes. She didn't budge. He'd hoped she'd wake so they could pick up where Dave had interrupted.

No chance of that now.

He let out a deep sigh. Alan had told him to man up and face the issue head-on. He'd been testing the waters, reminding her they had no commitment. He'd hoped for a reaction, a discussion, but above all he'd wanted denial.

But she hadn't taken the bait. She either said nothing or confirmed his no-commitment liturgy and that made him uncomfortable. Why couldn't she commit to him? What was wrong? He tackled problems head-on, so why not this one? Because...all her hesitancy made him afraid that if he pushed too hard she'd leave.

He knew Alan was right.

He kissed her forehead. He'd put off talking to her until this weekend.

He didn't want to turn back now. He wanted forever. With Margot.

He was going to propose to her tomorrow. There were still things he needed to do.

Do. The list. Shit. He closed his eyes. He had to speak to the driver and... He gave up and drifted off to sleep.

♥♥♥

Margot relaxed poolside trying to get rid of her throbbing headache.

It had been late morning when she'd gotten out of bed. Morgan was gone. His note said he'd see her about lunchtime. Unable to face breakfast, she'd put on the one-piece bathing suit with the plunging neckline and cut-out back that Morgan had given her before they went to Star Island. According to the weekend program, most of the wedding guests were off hiking. For her, lying out in the late-morning sun was as close to nature as she wanted to get.

The rustic setting of the inn's pool was inviting. The area appeared more like a grotto than the typical chlorine-blue oblong. Large smooth fieldstones rimmed the saltwater pool. Water sluiced over the six-foot-high waterfall at the far end. Native shrubs dotted the pool deck and were complemented by the Adirondack chairs and lounges scattered around.

She took a deep breath of the clean mountain air and settled back. If she stayed real still, her headache retreated to a dull thud. In a haze, she drifted off into a light sleep.

"Good morning." Margot jolted at the sudden interruption that set off a brutal pounding in her head. As sweet as the voice was, she swore the woman had a megaphone focused at her ear. If she kept her head still, perhaps the pounding would let up. Light was another issue. She adjusted her dark glasses and the wide brim of her straw hat, hoping to hide behind them before she closed her eyes and sank further back into the lounge chair, trying to disappear.

Her silent treatment crumbled under the weight of the woman's stare. Shit, it was the same silent treatment, soaked in a good dose of guilt, her mother used when she wanted her to do something.

Besides, the woman was part of either Viv's or Gabe's family. She could at least be hospitable.

"Morning," she mumbled, hoping the woman wouldn't say anything else. Or better yet, go away.

"Beautiful day, isn't it?" The scrape of the lounge chair next to her was startling.

"Jeez," she muttered. She didn't want to be sociable. Why'd she say anything?

"Are you with the wedding? It seems to have taken over the inn. You can't walk anywhere without bumping into a wedding guest or someone from the wedding party. I'm Agnes, by the way. I didn't catch your name." The woman wanted to talk. That was the last thing she wanted.

"Leave the girl alone." She flinched at the gravelly voice that came from Agnes's direction. "Can't you see she doesn't want to be disturbed?" the feisty old man scolded the woman. Another chair scraped the pool deck.

Oh no, there were two of them.

She peeked through small slits, her eyes adjusting to the light as she glanced around the pool. All the other chairs were empty; no towels draped on the backs or seats reserving them, either. If she could, she'd stand up and move but she didn't want to offend anyone from either family.

She sat up straighter and her stomach growled. Maybe she could flag the waiter for something to eat? She glanced at the bar. Still no one in sight.

"Nonsense, Albert. I'm just being sociable." The woman made herself comfortable.

Crap, she was settling in for the afternoon.

"You're a busybody and pain in the ass, if you ask me," Albert interjected. That caught Margot's attention.

She peered out from under the protection of her hat. His hand rested on Agnes's. That surprised her. His gentle touch didn't match his attitude. There was more beneath the surface even though his face was red and screwed up in anger. Agnes wasn't fazed. "The woman's trying to rest," he yelled in a whisper—if a person could yell in a whisper.

She had a hard time trying not to laugh.

Agnes huffed and glared at the man. "Well, I'm not asking you." Her voice lost its sweet nature, but Margot didn't miss the stink-eye Agnes gave him. Their argument made her a bit uncomfortable but she got the feeling their out-in-the-open quarreling was their usual routine and wasn't anything unique. Agnes returned her focus to Margot, a sweet smile back on her face.

"As I was saying, I didn't catch your name—"

She may as well resign herself. They were here to stay.

"You deaf as well as a royal pain? She didn't give you her name." He stared right at Margot. "Did you?" After being spoken about as if she wasn't there, his direct question caught her by surprise. She opened her mouth to speak but nothing came out. "Not speaking. Good for you." He smiled and rubbed Agnes's arm. "See, Agnes, she's mute. Can't speak. Probably deaf, too." He sat back in the chair.

Agnes waved him away and leaned toward Margot. "Don't pay any attention to him. In a few minutes he won't remember he's seen us."

She took off her glasses. "My name's Margot." She stared at Agnes. Her grandmother came to mind. She sniffed the air—strawberry and pink jasmine with a hint of green mandarin—ah, Miss Dior perfume, her grandmother's favorite. Margot sat back. So did Agnes, a pleased expression on her face.

"Her name is Margot," she called out. "She's not deaf or dumb. She's quite nice, actually." The woman's eyes hadn't left hers.

"Yeah? And how the hell do you know all that from getting her name?" The man struggled to his feet. "If you're going to yap all afternoon I'm going to find me some peace and quiet and you, Margot, are welcome to join me. You won't get any rest with her jabbering." He stalked off toward the inn's lobby. Not exactly like her grandfather, although he did wear his pants up high with suspenders like Old Pop, but that was the only similarity. Albert was a character. Agnes made nothing of his outburst so she relaxed.

"At last," Agnes said. "You're not married or engaged." Agnes nodded toward her left hand. Margot forced herself to not pull it away. "Smart girl. You've got to be careful. There are men," Agnes bent close to her and whispered, "all men, really, think with their penis."

Agnes and Albert. That was a picture she needed to erase from her mind real quick. But it was stuck there. Margot's fingers touched her throat. It was a bit flushed as heat raced up her neck and settled in her cheeks. Agnes sat back.

"Did I startle you, dear? I call them as I see them. Love is in the air at a wedding. It's like the flu. People you would never think to marry look good." Agnes cast a glance toward the inn's lobby doors. Was that how Agnes viewed Albert? No, she didn't believe that for a moment. They argued but their gentle touches spoke louder—they cared for each other.

"I know the signs. Albert proposed the day my sister got married. It was like this wedding but in Vermont. He was all lovey dovey and I was taken in by the day and his uniform. I said yes. Since the family was around, we got our license and were married the next day. I had the same minister and the same flowers. My sister wanted me to wear her wedding gown, but I wanted to get married in my uniform. I was an army nurse. The day was perfect. Albert was perfect. Life was going to be perfect. The next day Albert shipped out to Korea. That was in 1953, sixty-two years ago." Margot didn't miss the despair on Agnes's face. She was relieved it wasn't regret. Realization hit her. Albert—this Albert—wasn't the man she married. He was locked somewhere inside himself. Was he slipping away little by little? Did the real Albert break out every so often?

"Well, no sense crying over something you can't change." Agnes let out a heavy sigh and patted Margot's hand. "Just be careful you don't get caught up in this wedding whirl. I've been watching."

"And what have you seen?" Margot wasn't a gossip, but it was laughable how Agnes lit up at the opportunity to tell all she knew. She needed to know to which family Agnes was related.

Those eyes had Gabe written all over them. Yeah, the more she considered it, the more she thought Agnes had to be from Gabe's side of the family.

"Well," Agnes scooted her chair closer, "that young man there," and nodded toward the inn door.

Margot turned to spot who the young man in question was. No one was at the door except Morgan and Nikki, the inn owner.

"He can't keep his hands off anyone. Those two have been sneaking around and meeting in strange places." Stunned by Agnes's words, Margot could only nod. "Last night she pulled him into her office and this morning she practically dragged him down the drive. I couldn't hear what they were saying, but one minute Nikki's in tears and the next she's screaming at him." Margot couldn't curb the flash of anger or the flare of heat that raced through her. Jealous. She didn't have a green bone in her body.

"Albert and I have been coming here for years and know Nikki and Nate Flynn real well. She would never do anything rash."

Margot settled back and smoldered as she watched Morgan and Nikki with their heads together. She didn't think anything of the two of them laughing, not even when Nikki put her hand on Morgan's arm, but she wanted to jump out of her chair when Morgan covered her hand with his.

"I tell you it must be that man."

Agnes hadn't taken her eyes off the pair. "I can't tell what they're saying but it looks all cozy to me."

Cozy? She stared at Morgan, her stomach in turmoil—and not from the little pink things she'd been drinking last night.

Wait, he'd been one of the organizers of last night's party. And Gabe had Morgan doing all sorts of errands for him today. It must be related to the wedding. What else would they be talking about? She let Agnes provoke her. It was clear his head-bumping with Nikki was about the weekend. She stretched her neck for a better view. Morgan was in attorney mode right down to his glare and crossed arms in front of his puffed chest. He'd taken great care in developing that stance. It made him appear bigger and broader. Although he wasn't a trial attorney, his presence at the bargaining table was fearsome. She'd seen him in action once, but if she were in a court battle she'd want him on her side. She was dizzy with relief. She didn't want to admit the idea that he might be interested in someone else unsettled her more than her already defiant stomach.

"And she's not the only woman he's been flirting with." Agnes's conspiratorial tone made her jerk her head toward the woman.

"What do you mean?" She struggled to keep her voice even. Their relationship was solid. She glanced at Morgan as he smiled at Nikki. Oh God, their relationship was falling apart in front of her. Unable to sit still, she licked her lips and swung her legs to the ground, ready to leave. She didn't want to listen but she couldn't leave, either.

"I was talking to him in the lobby last night. He impressed me as such a nice man. Morgan Stuart is his name. When the woman came in he acted surprised to see her. At first I didn't think anything of it. I mean, you see people at weddings you haven't seen in years and can't place them. But this? This was different. The woman tried to pretend she didn't see him, even hid her face. As if standing there right next to him he wouldn't notice her."

Morgan wouldn't… She stopped herself. Last night, during the party, the phone call…he'd said he had to take care of something.

"I saw him later in the lobby and watched them. She searched around looking for someone. At first I thought she was looking for someone to save her. But when she led him into the lounge—which was closed, by the way— I realized she wanted to get him alone."

Agnes had it all wrong. The woman must be a wedding guest. Secret rendezvous weren't Morgan's style. He'd have an explanation, she was positive. That was when reality hit her. He didn't have to give her an explanation. He'd been reminding her they didn't have a commitment—as recently as last night.

"I've got to go," Agnes said. "Before Albert makes a scene." Albert leaned out the door and waved for Agnes to join him. "See you at dinner. It's going to be such a lovely wedding." Agnes gathered her things and left.

"You still bothering Margie?" Albert said within

earshot, playfully scolding Agnes as the woman reached the door.

"Her name is Margot," Agnes said before she walked into the lobby.

Albert threw his arms in the air and followed Agnes's lead. Nikki held the door for them. Morgan walked toward her.

Could Agnes be right? No commitment. He'd been stressing that since…since they came back from Star Island.

Was there someone else?

She searched his face for anything that told her things between them had changed. His stride was easy and his smile was warm. He gave her an all-was-right-with-the-world look. Or was that what she wanted to think? The up-and-down conversation with Agnes made her head hurt. She didn't know how to react to him.

"How do you feel?" he asked, sitting in Agnes's empty chair. "I thought you'd sleep through the morning."

He appeared relaxed without a care in the world. She bit the inside of her cheek, weighing whether to tell him what was on her mind.

"You okay? You look like you have the weight of the world on your shoulders. All you have to do tonight is walk down the aisle. It's a rehearsal."

"I'm fine. Just a dull headache. Agnes talked my ear off. I don't know which family she belongs to but she and Albert are really a pair." She chuckled and struggled to bury her anxiety. She needed to think this through and decide what to do.

"I have aspirin upstairs." He sat back in the chair, closed his eyes and took in the sun.

She glanced at her watch. Noon. She had to dial in to the Boyles auction at two.

"The wedding band canceled," he said, still playing the sun worshipper.

"What?" She shot up in her chair. "What are they going to do?" Viv had contracted with the group months ago. They were up and coming and she was adamant about having them play.

"Relax. I told you last night." He sat up, finished with his sun prayers. "I was going over a legal issue with Nikki when the band manager called her. It seems Viv and Gabe weren't answering their phones."

Last night? She didn't remember him—oh yes, she spoke to him but she'd be dammed if she could bring back the conversation. She gathered her things.

"You remember that special event I helped Eloise put together." Morgan's sister-in-law was the executive director of The North Star Project, an agency advocating against human trafficking.

Her brow creased in deep concentration. "What does that have to do with the wedding?" Morgan had put together a high-profile fund-raiser which included a contract for Tara Graham, the Grammy Award winning singer-song writer, to entertain.

"I saw Tara in the lobby last night. I was surprised when she walked in but not as surprised as she was to find me here. We caught up and I told her what happened with the musicians."

She was putting the bottle of suntan lotion, which she didn't get a chance to put on, into her bag and stopped. "Are you telling me that Tara Graham, *the* Tara Graham, is performing at the wedding?" Her stomach let out a loud rumble. Agnes must've seen Morgan with Tara last night. Her anxiety level plummeted.

"Yes, she is."

"You spoke to her about it last night?" It was a question rather than a statement. She squeezed the bottle of lotion so hard that it exploded all over her. Morgan was quick to grab a pool towel from the nearby stack and wiped her down, which made it worse but the damage was already done. She smelled like a coconut.

"Yes, and she had a legal issue. I gave her advice on what to discuss with her attorney." He was still mopping up globs of lotion.

She put the bottle into her bag and her stomach let out another rumble. "Have you eaten?" Morgan asked. She shook her head. "Me neither. Come on." He threw the towel into the bin. "I'll split a piece of apple pie with you. That should hold us for now."

She slung the beach bag onto her shoulder and stepped into her sandals. "Hot and with vanilla ice cream." Her world, which had been off kilter since last night, came back into focus.

He put his arm around her and squeezed. "Hot apple pie with vanilla ice cream it is." They headed to the lobby café.

♥♥♥

"You want the last of the ice cream?" Morgan's fork was poised over the plate. He had an I-really-want-that-last-spoonful look in his eye.

"No, you can have it." His spoon scooped up the ice cream before she finished her sentence. She smiled as he wiped the last bit of the dessert from his mouth then checked her watch.

"It's one thirty. I need to dial in to the Boyles auction. By the way, do you think we'll have time to explore the falls tomorrow? Viv told me it's a must see."

He folded his napkin and placed it on the table.

"Yes. We'll go right after you get all glamorized with the rest of the girls. I have to meet Tara. You want to wait for me here or in our room?" He was on his feet.

"You go on ahead. I want to get ready for the call. I'll meet you upstairs." He left her at the table and walked across to the banquet room. She drained the last of her iced tea and made her way toward the elevator. The airport van must've arrived. Suitcases and garment bags cluttered the lobby. A long line of new guests choked the registration desk. Nikki and her daughter Noelle were busy getting people registered.

"No, that won't work. I'm Gabe's aunt Bea and must be in the room next to my sister." The woman was adamant.

Margot navigated past the crowd. What a zoo.

"Mom, why can't I have my own room?" A young girl stomped her foot and glared at her mother.

"Because you're twelve years old and you'll stay with your father and me. End of story."

A commotion on the other side of the lobby involving two women grabbed her attention. Was that the sheriff? Yes, it was, and with a bloody nose.

"This is the medical emergency," a third woman said. She turned to see Davina, Viv's friend, scurrying toward the bleeding man. Margot couldn't keep up with the score card. She'd ask Viv or Davina what happened later.

Jostled by the crowd, she struggled with her oversized beach bag to maneuver around the crush of people and reached the elevator. "Hold it, please." She rushed inside. "Thanks," she said before she turned around.

"The pleasure is all mine." She froze as the deep velvet sound washed over her. She'd know that voice anywhere. Her heart was beating wildly and she had a hard time controlling it. A slow pirouette brought her face-to-face with Zack Douglas. His fair complexion, blond good looks and hazel eyes had made her swoon in college. They'd remained together through grad school but as the years passed their lives went in different directions. She got involved in her parents' antiques shop and Zack, an engineer, tried to find his place in the world but for him it was elusive and his restlessness frustrated both of them. They grew further apart until nothing was left between them. He'd stepped out of her life and away from all their friends. It was sad but not devastating. Well, not too devastating.

"Hi, Zack." She found her voice as the elevator stopped on the second floor and they got out. At one time, she'd had a million questions she'd wanted to ask him, but now she couldn't think of one. The opening strains of "Smooth" caught her attention and she smiled. It had been their song.

He took his cell phone out of his pocket and checked the display. "Sorry, I have to take this." He didn't wait for her to answer. "Dr. Douglas, how can I help you?"

Doctor. That took her by surprise but only the drastic shift from engineering. *Concerned* and *lifesaver* were terms that fit him. If anyone needed something, anything, you called Zack. He ended his call.

"I'm glad I bumped into you." He sniffed the air. "You smell—"

"Like a coconut. I had a run-in with a bottle of suntan lotion. I had no idea you were coming." She didn't know that Gabe and Zack kept in touch.

"I didn't, either, until I bumped into Gabe in the old neighborhood. I've been overseas for the past five years and returned to the states last week. We spent a few hours reminiscing and catching up on what everyone is doing." So this was spontaneous. How like Gabe to offer the invitation. "Actually, you and Gabe are the only people who know I'm here. He mentioned you've taken over the antiques shop and turned out to be quite the art collector."

"Only for other people." Seeing him made her insides flutter as they did when she found an exceptional antique. Or was it Agnes or the little pink drinks that had her stomach in motion? There was something about Zack that…

Little by little, the awkwardness of seeing him after all these years faded and he was an old friend with whom she'd lost contact. Nothing else.

"I'm glad for you." He squeezed her hand. "I want to catch up and hear all about it but I have to take care of this." He held up his cell phone before he slipped it back into his pocket. She didn't notice any hint of apprehension in his touch or the awakening of any dormant romantic feelings. No, the romance was reserved for Morgan. But she did get the sense that Zack was confident and grounded, set on his path. "I'm sorry I have to go. Can we speak later?"

"Sure," she said. His face lit with a wide smile. She smiled back.

"Thanks." He dropped her hand. "I'll see you later." He headed right, his cell phone already in his hand.

She turned left and took a few steps before she peered over her shoulder. He was gone. She was excited at reconnecting and catching up. A lot had happened in ten years. She continued on to her room. That was pleasant, two old friends meeting. Then why had she looked at his ring finger for a wedding band, which he didn't have? To know if he'd made a commitment?

She entered her room and put her bag near the desk. The aroma of coconut was overpowering. The bathing suit was exchanged for a lacy cover-up. She grabbed her tablet. It was ten to two. Morgan's message to George

Hughes was at the top of her inbox. He had given George all the information he needed about the auction and accolades about her. Morgan was one of her biggest supporters. She dialed in to the auction.

"Good afternoon. You've reached Boyles Auction House. This is Christina. How may I help you?"

"Hi, Chris, Margot here," she said as she opened her folder, checked her bidder number—six thirty-eight—and pulled out the auction catalog. She took one last glance at the rare fourteenth-century Italian *cassone*. The dome-top chest with painted panels was valued at forty-five thousand dollars. The provenance was all in order. According to George Hughes, the chest had been part of the Fayne Manor tower room furnishings.

"There's a late addition to the lot in which you're interested, an early seventeenth-century cradle. It's in excellent condition and has been valued at ninety-five hundred dollars. It's intricately carved wood with a gold polychrome. I've sent you a picture. The price range for the lot is twenty-two thousand and fifty-four thousand five hundred dollars."

"Yes, I saw this yesterday but you'd already gone for the day. It looks beautiful." They were selling the *cassone* and cradle together. She had contacted George Hughes with the additional item right after she got Chris's email. He was eager to have them both. If she could close this deal it would be a real coup. These were museum-quality pieces. She had to play this right. Chris may be a good friend but her allegiance was to "the House."

"I think there are two other dealers who may be interested in the same lot. They're here on the premises. While these pieces are good, we have several others in today's auction that surpass them. And before you say anything, I've already pointed that out to the other bidders."

"Thanks." She knew Chris was right. One item in particular made everything else pale. It was unfortunate that the piece went on the block before the Fayne Manor pieces. She was concerned that the losing bidders, who hadn't spent their money, may find the lot she wanted interesting.

Her phone buzzed with a text message. George was excited and wished her luck. He was on the line listening to the auction. With the addition of the cradle, he had increased her spending limit to sixty-five thousand dollars. The family he represented wanted to restore the manor in the seventeenth-century style and was dedicated to "bringing home" as many original pieces as possible.

While she waited for the auction to begin, she browsed through the papers in her folder and put her hand on Gabe and Viv's invitation. What was it doing in this folder? Another one of her filing secrets. Her finger traced the satin-finished border. For a moment she imagined her name and Morgan's engraved on it instead of Gabe and Viv. That wasn't going to happen. It wasn't so bad to go on as they had. She stuffed the card back into her folder.

Had Morgan grown too accustomed to her being around? They did live together. She leaned back in the chair. She didn't have to give up. Or make it easy for him to walk away. She needed to put the spark back into their relationship. *That's it, Margot, pull out all the stops tonight.* The strappy sundress for the rehearsal along with her hair down…he wouldn't have a chance. She hoped.

"Margot, they're starting." She straightened in the chair and pushed all thoughts of Morgan from her mind.

Margot listened to get a sense of the bidding climate, what to expect on the items she wanted. The auctioneer passed the first three items. They hadn't reached the reserve price, the minimum price the consignor requested. It wasn't unusual. The pieces would be offered at a private sale or at the next auction. They were all fine pieces. She had examined them when she visited Boyles on Wednesday at the presale exhibit. But the passes did indicate that everyone was holding on to their money and waiting for the Louis XVI *cartonnier*. The writing desk and cabinet was in magnificent condition and was valued at over one hundred ninety thousand dollars. It was next up.

"Margot, they're having mechanical difficulty bringing the *cartonnier* to the block. Mr. Boyle instructed the handlers to bring up the *cassone* and cradle instead of waiting." Her heart pounded from the adrenaline rush. It happened at every auction. But this was different; this small change in the schedule could work to her advantage. At least she hoped it could.

Bidding opened at twenty thousand, two hundred and fifty dollars and went up in thousand dollar increments. Margot was in the mix. When the price reached thirty thousand, two hundred and fifty dollars the bidding slowed. This is what she was waiting for.

"Thirty-five thousand, five hundred," she told Chris. The other bidders were silent.

"Going once, going twice. Final call—"

"Thirty-seven thousand," a bidder called out. She waited for the final call.

"Forty thousand, eight hundred seventy-five," she told Chris. She could hear a flurry of noise on Chris's side.

"You appear to have annoyed the gentleman in the front. He's shaking his head no." Her adrenaline, which was already racing, pumped harder.

"Going once, going twice..." The auctioneer paused. Margot stood up, waiting for the final call. "Sold," he brought down the hammer, "to number six thirty-eight." A scream built inside her but at the last second she slapped her hand over her mouth. Her phone pinged with a text. George sent his congratulations when the hammer hit. The key turned in the door.

"Congratulations, Margot." Chris was as excited as she was. "I'll take care of the paperwork and have it all on your desk Monday morning." Margot answered George's message. With her twenty percent commission she'd still saved him sixteen thousand dollars.

"Thanks, Chris. Have a great weekend."

Morgan opened the door and she danced over to him. From the look on his face she had no doubt that he expected her to still be on the call. She gave Morgan a big kiss. "Ask me how we did." She pranced out of his reach.

"How'd we do?" He came in, emptied his pockets on the dresser and took out his clothes for the evening.

"Boyles always amazes me." She closed her tablet as she went into the bathroom. "I've already gotten a message from George. Two Fayne Manor pieces of furniture are going home. He's pleased. We saved his client a lot of money." She grabbed her comb and pulled it through her hair to detangle the nest that had settled there. Should she tell him about Zack? No, it was nothing important. "How did things go with Tara?" Her hair was a bit wild but at least it was tangle free when she went back into the room.

She turned to face him when he didn't answer. Her breath caught. His shirt was off and he had that smile that made her bones weak. She stood mesmerized against the bathroom door.

"I love it when you wear your hair down, all loose and wild." His voice purred as his fingers raked through her hair. He braced his hand on the wall behind her then leaned forward, closing the distance between them to inches. Her eyes fluttered as his breath brushed across her face. She said nothing and instead she told him she loved him with her eyes.

How did he do it? One minute she was calm and cool, the next she was hungry and burning. His soft lips nibbled and tickled her ear. His face loomed so close she could see the silver flecks in his blue eyes. Her heart banged against her chest. His breath against her neck was warm. The rest of her, the parts he loved, were hot. His lips came down on hers and captured them in a tender but fierce possession. A moment of panic spiked through her like an arrow, but disappeared under an all-consuming rush of heat.

God, she wanted a commitment and only Morgan Stuart would do.

♥♥♥

Morgan set her drink—seltzer with lime—on the cocktail table on the terrace.

"Isn't this a rehearsal?" Margot asked him in hushed tones. He should have known Viv and Gabe would be unconventional. It was their style.

"There's been a change in plans. Let me find out what's happening. I'll be right back." He walked over to Gabe and the knot of men standing by the gazebo.

"We can't do the rehearsal. The gazebo won't be ready until tomorrow so we're going to plan B, the Cliff Notes version. You'll be walking down the aisle with your wife or," he stared at Morgan, "significant other. Since there're four couples, this shouldn't be difficult." Gabe handed each man a piece of paper. He opened the folded paper with *M and M* printed on it in bold letters. "Morgan, you and Margot are first down the aisle."

Morgan nodded. When he looked up, a blond

stranger sat with Margot. He didn't recognize who it was but wasn't surprised. Margot's and Viv's families went back a long time. He was the newcomer at ten years and still didn't know everyone.

"I've been busting Gabe's chops telling him we're going to dance down the aisle, record it and put it on the Internet." Gabe's brother couldn't stop laughing. They made their way to the bar and ordered beers. "Jeez, I haven't seen Zack Douglas in years." The bottle of beer in Morgan's hand hung frozen in midair. He didn't need to see where Gabe's brother was looking. Zack was with Margot. "We're playing a short round of golf tomorrow. You joining us?" Gabe's brother asked.

"No, Margot wants to go to the falls tomorrow. Viv told her it was a special place," Morgan said.

"You're cutting it close. The wedding's tomorrow late afternoon. And don't let my wife know you're going to the falls or she'll have me there, too." The two shared a laugh although Morgan didn't feel like laughing. Gabe's brother gave him a heavy pat on the back and was lost in the crowd.

He watched Margot and Zack as he drank his beer, controlling his impulse to go up to Zack Douglas and tell him to get lost. Zack had his chance and Margot was his now.

That led to a quick and disturbing notion. Was she his? Had she been holding out these ten years for Zack?

Wait, he told himself as he got his emotions under control. He raked his hand through his hair. He knew she loved him. It was in the way she spoke to him, the way she looked at him, the way she touched him and the way they made love. There was no faking that.

No, he was sure she loved him. Why had she insisted on no commitment? Had it been Zack all along? He'd make sure one way or the other. Finishing his beer, he put the bottle on the bar, got a seltzer with lime and went to their table.

When he reached Margot, he put her drink in front of her and his hand on her shoulder. He knew he made a blatant statement. That's what he wanted Zack to see. He waited two, maybe three heartbeats. He saw no evidence of aggression or surprise on Zack's face. Margot put her hand on his and he relaxed a notch. "Morgan. This is Zack Douglas." Zack stood up and extended his hand.

"Good to meet you, Morgan." He took the outstretched hand. "Margot and I have been catching up."

"Zack." They turned around at Gabe motioning Zack to come over.

"One minute, Gabe." Zack returned his attention to Margot. "It was a nice surprise seeing you in the elevator this afternoon." Elevator? He had his game face on but it didn't help when he saw Margot wince. She hadn't mentioned that to him. He was on slippery ground. What else hadn't she told him?

"Zack." Gabe was more insistent.

"Coming." Zack turned to them. "Sorry. I've got to go. Nice meeting you, Morgan." He picked up Margot's hand and squeezed it before he left.

Morgan sat beside her. For once he didn't know what to say or where to start. His cool exterior hid his biggest fear—that Margot might walk away.

"What did Gabe want?"

He showed her the number scribbled on an index card. "We're first down the aisle. When we reach the gazebo, I go to the right and you go to the left."

"That's simple enough." Margot was more at ease than she had been in days. Was that because of Zack? The auction? Their lovemaking? He twisted in knots. "It was good to see Zack. He's so different, so settled. He's a doctor."

Good for him. He didn't give a crap about what Zack had become. *Careful, get those emotions under control.*

He dug deep and strapped on his attorney armor and masked his face with indifference. Silence was his best weapon. He let the silence grow, knowing she'd be compelled to fill it. He wouldn't have to wait long.

"Come to think of it, I did most of the talking. He didn't say much." She was deep in concentration as her thoughts crisscrossed her face. He watched and waited. With each moment his heart squeezed tighter. Would she walk away from everything they'd built together? He didn't want to lose her. "I'll make sure he does the talking when we meet up later." She glanced past his shoulder. "Gabe's mother is waving. I better get over there. Oh, Agnes and Albert are with her. I suspected they were from Gabe's family." She got up and kissed him on his forehead and left.

"Meet up later," he repeated to himself. *Did Zack think he could just walk back into her life after ten years? Ten years?* he screamed inside his head. He let out a deep breath, puffing out his cheeks trying to ease the knot that tightened in his chest. He closed his eyes and knew he could lose her.

Morgan walked around the room saying hello to people, talking about the local baseball game and the potential for the football teams this fall, but he couldn't get Margot and Zack out of his mind. She was planted beside Zack at a remote cocktail table the entire evening. He was used to them working the room separately on occasion but tonight he wanted her with him. He weighed whether to join them or give her space. He left them alone. Give them their time together. But he loved her and if he had to, he'd fight for her, hard…and dirty, if necessary.

He'd do anything to keep her.

♥♥♥

"I hope you had a good time last night. I saw you talking to Zack. All evening," Viv said to Margot in the morning at the spa.

"Yeah, we were catching up." Margot got her things together to go. She hadn't been aware of how long she and Zack had been talking.

"Where are you going? I thought we'd spend the afternoon together in the spa." Viv stood there, wearing a white terry cloth robe that said *Bride* on the back and her hands on her hip. She gave Margot a sour face.

"I asked Morgan to take me to the falls." She got into a casual sundress and sandals. "Besides I've been saunaed, massaged and had a mani-pedi."

"It's a romantic spot. Are you going to propose to him?" Viv laughed.

"No, don't be silly. Why would we want to change a good thing? I'll see you before the ceremony." She should've spent more time with Morgan last night. One minute it was early evening, and the next the bartender announced last call. Morgan had gone up to their room hours before she did and was asleep when she came in.

She kissed Viv and met Morgan in the lobby.

"Ready? Your carriage awaits." He gave her a deep bow that made her laugh while he pushed open the inn door.

She stopped laughing. "You weren't joking." In front of her was a horse and carriage. Todd, Nikki's handsome handyman, stood ready to help them in.

She stared at Morgan and was consumed with guilt

for spending so much time with Zack the night before.

It could make him declare himself for her or it could backfire and make him walk away. She hadn't slept last night. She got the idea after six vodka shots and catching a glimpse of Morgan's hangdog expression. It seemed like a good idea at the time. Let him see someone else interested in her. Maybe then he would make a commitment.

Now she had second thoughts.

He'd left to go up to their room without telling her. She'd panicked when she couldn't find him. It wasn't until the bartender said last call that Viv told her Morgan had left a few hours earlier. Several times she wanted to wake him and confess she had monopolized Zack on purpose. Instead she watched him sleep and cuddled next to him, fearing it was her last night with him.

He helped her into the carriage, where they found a basket filled with champagne and hors d'oeuvres.

The small canapés were gone and he'd poured the last glass of champagne when they reached the bottom of the falls. They stood by the railing enjoying the view. The sun painted everything with a rich patina. Even the spray of water was tinged with gold. The mist danced before it settled back onto the river and was carried away. It took her breath away. She watched the water while she held on to Morgan.

He pulled her around and stared into her eyes.

"Marry me."

She stood stone-still, her hand on his chest. Had she heard him right? There was a deep rumble in his chest. "Are you speechless?" His voice quivered.

He was nervous. She was scared.

He asked her to marry him.

What had she done? These were the words she wanted to hear, but she couldn't say yes, not now. Would he still want her if he knew she made him jealous to make him propose? She looked at his hand. He held an open box. The sun caught the diamond ring and sent flashes of a rainbow into the mist. It all melded together. The ring, the falls, Morgan. It was beautiful.

"Do you need time before you answer?" He waited a heartbeat. "I would think that ten years is time enough to, you know, to make a commitment."

Her head popped up. Commitment.

She was surprised he couldn't hear her heart pounding. An agonizing moment ticked past.

"Of course I'll marry you," she blurted out. His face lit with excitement. He held her tight and she forced a smile. She was empty. Tears tracked down her cheeks. She should be elated. This was what she wanted. But she'd tricked him. There was no joy in that. "Let's not take the thunder away from Viv and Gabe. It's their wedding."

Would he buy her stalling tactic? She needed time to tell him the truth. She had no intention of rekindling her relationship with Zack. Morgan was all she spoke about last night. For her it had always been Morgan. It would always be Morgan. For now, this moment, she wanted to enjoy being engaged to him. Maybe she could find a way to make this right. "It's a wonderful proposal, and the ring is more than I could ever hope for. I love you. I've loved you forever." She threw her arms around him and kissed him. She wished with all her heart he loved her enough to forgive her deception.

"I know we haven't discussed getting married and you're right about Viv and Gabe. We'll keep this to ourselves for now." She tucked her head beneath his chin and worried whether things would be the same after she confessed.

"Excuse me," Todd said. "Congratulations. I hate to

break this up but it's time to get back to the inn."

Morgan led her to the carriage.

The carriage wasn't going at a breakneck speed but they hurried along. She sat cuddled in his arms and enjoyed the excitement of being engaged. The landscape rushed by until they turned into the driveway and pulled to a stop at the inn's entrance.

"It's time to get into my tux. I'm changing with the other ushers." He kissed her nose. "See you in a few minutes." He hurried off to meet the other men.

She rushed up the steps. When she opened her purse to take out the key she stared at the small box.

She was numb getting ready. Damn it, she should have told him everything, and that Zack meant nothing to her. She touched up her makeup, changed her dress and slipped on her shoes. A quick comb through her hair and she was ready. She sat on the bed, took out the box and fit the ring on her finger. Maybe he'd laugh at her silliness with Zack. But she wasn't laughing. She was disappointed...with herself.

She put the ring back in the box, pulled out her phone and called him. She'd explain about Zack. Tell him that she was trying to...make him jealous with her old boyfriend. Oh God, that sounded horrible even to her.

"Margot?" *Go ahead*, she told herself. *Tell him. You created this little mess, clean it up*.

"Morgan."

"I can't hear you. There's a lot of noise here. Is everything all right?" Her chin quivered so much she couldn't speak.

She closed her eyes and struggled to get the words out. "I can't marry you."

"What'd you say? Honey, I can't hear you."

"I...can't marry you," she shouted as tears ran down her face.

"Wait, I'll be right there." She didn't want him to come to the room.

"No, I'm coming." She ended the call before she started sobbing. That was the coward's way to tell him. Commitment or not, he deserved more than a phone call. Her hand shook as she put the ring box in her purse. She picked up her flowers and headed for the garden.

When she came through the lounge, her plan to tell him everything fell apart. She couldn't face him. If she told him what she'd done she was sure he would break it off with her. But she couldn't live with herself and accept his ring if she didn't tell him. How was she going to get through the rest of the day?

"You look lovely." She glanced up at Zack.

"Zack?" she whispered. "Zack!" She stared at his priest's collar. If he was surprised at her reaction he kept it well hidden. "I thought you were a doctor." Now she was humiliated. She'd waved her reunion with Zack in front of Morgan and the man was a…

"I have a PhD in engineering. They use my title at school. I wanted to tell you about it last night but you didn't give me a chance. You never stopped talking about Morgan."

"When did you become a minister?" Now his manner last night made sense. If anything, the more she spoke about Morgan, the more she understood how much she loved him.

"It's a long story, too long to tell now. Suffice it to say that while I worked on my PhD I was involved in an engineering project for the church and found my calling. I've combined both my loves. Now I'm the chair of the engineering department at the seminary."

"I'm glad for you." And she was. She stared at him. He'd been searching for something, trying to find his place. He'd found his passion and he was at peace. Okay, that was getting a bit too ecclesiastical, but he was. He'd made his commitment.

"I have to marry a bride and groom. May I take you to Morgan? I liked him after you and I spoke. I got to know him this morning. We had a good talk while you girls were getting glamorized." She stared at him, startled. Morgan hadn't told her he spoke to Zack. "He loves you and he has for a long time. You were all he talked about." Her eyes widened in surprise that Morgan had spoken about her. "Why are you so surprised? Everyone knows you love each other. It's even evident to me." Noelle, the innkeeper's daughter, came in from the terrace and signaled to Zack. It was time for him to get in place.

"I'll see you after the ceremony." Zack went into the garden. She lowered into a nearby chair. What a mess she'd made of things.

"We'd better hurry. Everyone's seated." With Albert trailing behind her, Agnes rushed through the lounge. "Oh, Margot." She came to an abrupt stop where Margot sat. "You look lovely." Agnes tilted her face.

Margot turned away. She didn't want to speak to anyone.

"Why the long face? Has the old biddy been bending your ear again?" Albert gestured toward Agnes.

She stared at the two. They were the last people she wanted to talk to. She had to walk down the aisle in a few minutes. "No."

"Man trouble. That's what it is. It's written all over your face." Agnes sat next to her.

"Aw, jeez, Agnes, leave the girl alone. You've been pestering me to hurry, and now you want to sit." He screwed up his face in frustration.

"Be quiet." Agnes gave her attention to Margot. "Tell me what's wrong."

Margot studied them. What would they think of her? It couldn't be any worse than what she thought of herself.

"I led him to believe something that wasn't true. And he knows. Now he'll never trust me. Never." She fought to keep tears from falling. Her throat was raw and hot with the effort. All her dreams were going up in smoke.

Agnes glanced at Albert. "Get her a glass of water." He shuffled off without a complaint. Agnes patted her hand. "Start at the beginning. We'll figure out a solution."

"Morgan and I have been together a long time, ten years." She fidgeted with the ribbon on her bouquet. "From the start I told him I didn't want a commitment." She dropped the ribbon and searched Agnes's face, afraid at what she'd glimpse. "But I love him and want to spend the rest of my life with him."

"What's wrong with that?" Albert said. "Tell him you changed your mind. Hell, you women always change your minds. Agnes does it all the time." He handed her a glass of water.

"You don't understand. It's too late for that now. I tricked him. Last night I made him think I was interested in someone else. He proposed this afternoon." She took out the ring box and showed it to Agnes.

"Are you blind, girl? Can't you see anything?" Albert rubbed his chin. "The man loves you."

"You don't understand. He proposed because I tricked him. How can I base a marriage on that?"

Albert scratched his head and took the ring from Agnes. "I understand perfectly fine. You don't understand. How'd he get this fancy ring he gave you if he decided to ask you last night? He didn't get this out of any Cracker Jack box and there isn't a jeweler around for a hundred miles." He waved the ring at her. Agnes took the box out of his hand.

Startled and speechless, Margot stared at him. She hadn't considered that.

"Yeah, you tell me that." He fluttered his hands in

the air. "A stick has more common sense than you do and I'm not sure about the stick."

Agnes pulled a piece of paper out from under the velvet ring holder. "Your young man must have overlooked this. It says here he picked this up two weeks ago." Agnes's soft smile spread over her face. "He's been planning to ask you for some time." She tucked the box back into Margot's purse. He'd planned this all along. Commitment. Family. He wanted it as much as she did.

"Margot." Noelle came running into the lounge. "They're starting the processional."

"Go ahead now and hurry along," Agnes said, shooing Margot away.

"How can I thank you?" she said, getting to her feet.

"Marry him, and make him as miserable as she makes me," Albert said with a wink.

She hugged and kissed them both and hurried out to the garden, slipping in next to Morgan.

"I've been looking for you everywhere." That crease was in his forehead again.

"I have so much to tell you—"

"Well, not now." Noelle pulled Margot's skirt straight and fixed Morgan's tie. "You two, go."

"We'll talk later." He pulled her hand through his and brought her close. "You scared the hell out of me." Not as much as she had scared herself.

They walked down the aisle as Tara played the piano. A soft breeze rustled the trees and cooled the guests sitting in the late-afternoon sun. Fragrant roses filled the air. Colorful splashes of lady slippers completed the picture. The day was perfect. The bride and groom were perfect. And Margot cried all the way because Morgan loved her. Her day was perfect, too.

He put his arm around her waist and held her tight. She was glad he didn't say anything. He didn't have to.

She wanted him there, beside her, strong and steady. She knew she'd never leave him. "Morgan." He patted her hand and let go.

"Later. You go to the left. I go to the right." He gave her one of his smiles. The one he gave to her and no one else.

She fidgeted all through the ceremony. She needed to speak to Morgan and tell him everything.

"I now pronounce you man and wife." Zack leaned over to Gabe. "You may kiss the bride."

The guests applauded, took pictures, cheered at the same time. Viv and Gabe went up the aisle beaming. The other attendants followed behind them.

She walked toward the aisle and Morgan. She wanted him to know right this minute that she loved him and wanted him. While she waited for the couple before them to meet and start up the aisle, she took the ring out of her purse and put it on her finger.

She met him at the aisle and threaded her arm through his.

"I let you believe—"

"Shush. I know. When Gabe told me this morning that Zack was the minister, I figured it out." She didn't know if she was embarrassed or relieved. She chose to be relieved. "But I was no better. I waved the no-commitment flag in front of you hoping you'd tear it down. We've both been childish." Tear down the flag. She was speechless. She hadn't considered that. All along he wanted...her.

She placed her left hand over his. The ring caught the light and he stopped. They were halfway up the aisle. Everybody hushed. Viv, Gabe, Zack and the other attendants turned to see what was happening.

"Marry me," she whispered to him.

"I thought you'd never ask." She not only felt his

desire in the way he held his body, but she saw it in his eyes. She felt an insistent, all-consuming need for him to hold her.

He took her in his arms. The expression on his face was smoldering passion, love and devotion. The look Gabe gave to Viv. His face lit in his Bruce Willis smirk and she went weak in the knees. They gave each other a kiss that had *commitment* written all over it.

About…

Storyteller | Blogger | Creative Thinker | Dreamer
Good Sport | Teammate

You might be wondering what Ruth is about. Sit back and let her tell you.

She's happiest when she's telling stories either chatting in a group or writing them down. She loves to put her hero and heroine in tough situations and dare them to work it out—together, always together. They haven't disappointed her. Oh, they complain but in the end their love and relationships are stronger than ever.

While she keeps tormenting her druid knight, she's outlining a new series. The working title is the River of Time. It's about an elite technology security officer, whose job is to eliminate time travelers, but falls in love with a time traveling art appraiser and has to choose between his duty and his one chance for a timeless love. She loves this story line because it lets her stretch her contemporary voice while working in historic time periods. She thinks this is the best of both worlds.

For most of you, her contemporary side will be a surprise.

♥♥♥

Ruth would love to hear from you. Catch her on Twitter at @RuthACasie, you can drop her a line at Ruth@RuthACasie.com or visit her on FaceBook at www.facebook.com/RuthACasie. You can read more about Ruth online at www.RuthACasie.com where you can also join her newsletter.

♥♥♥

Want to read stories about a love so strong four hundred years couldn't keep Lord Arik and Rebeka apart? Then you'll want to read Ruth A. Casie's time travel series, the Druid Knight Stories.

♥♥♥

Knight of Rapture

He crossed the centuries to find her…

For months Lord Arik has been trying to find the right combination of runes to create the precise spell to rescue his wife, Rebeka, but the druid knight will soon discover that reaching her four hundred years in the future is only the beginning of his quest. He arrives in the 21st century to find her memory of him erased, his legacy on the brink of destruction, and traces of dark magick at every turn.

A threat has followed…

Bran, the dark druid, is more determined than ever to get his revenge. His evil has spread across the centuries. Arik will lose all. Time is his weapon, and he's made sure his plan leaves no one dear to Arik, in past or present, safe from the destruction.

But their enemy has overlooked the strongest magick of all…

Professor Rebeka Tyler is dealing with more than just a faulty memory. Ownership of Fayne Manor, her home, has been called into question. Convenient accidents begin happening putting those she cares for in the line of fire. And then there's the unexpected arrival of a strange man dressed like he belonged in a medieval fair—a man who somehow is always around when needed, and always on her mind. She doesn't know who to trust. But one thing is certain. Her family line and manor have survived for over eleven centuries. She won't let them fall, not on her watch… in any century.

♥♥♥

♥♥♥

Knight of Runes

When Lord Arik, a druid knight, finds Rebeka Tyler wandering his lands without protection, he swears to keep her safe. But Rebeka can take care of herself. When Arik sees her clash with a group of attackers using a strange fighting style, he's intrigued.

Rebeka is no ordinary seventeenth-century woman—she's travelled back from the year 2011, and she desperately wants to return to her own time. She poses as a scholar sent by the king to find out what's killing Arik's land. But as she works to decode the ancient runes that are the key to solving this mystery and sending her home, she finds herself drawn to the charismatic and powerful Arik.

As Arik and Rebeka fall in love, someone in Arik's household schemes to keep them apart, and a dark druid with a grudge prepares his revenge. Soon Rebeka will have to decide whether to return to the future or trust Arik with the secret of her time travel and her heart.

♥♥♥

♥♥♥

The Druid Knight Tales

Maximilian, the druid Grand Master, was given a year to find his soul mate. On the final day, the sacred mistletoe has shriveled and died—proclaiming his failure. He must do what no other Grand Master has done before and journey to meet with the Ancestors to formally relinquish his title.

Ellyn of Brodgar has the gift of healing. But each use of her magick, through a kiss, depletes her energy and brings her closer to death. Time is running out as she searches for a way to continue saving lives—especially her own.

Max and Ellyn are tossed into the Otherworld together—a place filled with magick and wonder, it's also fraught with danger, traps, and death. They have only until the third sunset to find the Ancestors, or be lost to the world forever. The domineering druid must work with the stubborn healer, not only for survival, but for the promise of the future—a future together.

Included an epilogue fifteen years later. See how the man destined for Max and Ellyn's daughter takes the first steps in becoming a druid knight.

Arik, son of Fendrel and Dimia, prepares for training with his adopted brother, Bran, setting into motion a ripple effect that will carry love, betrayal, and death across the centuries.

♥♥♥

In the mood for more paranormal romance by Ruth A. Casie? Check out her latest story, *The Guardian's Witch*, available now! www.RuthACasie.com/books.html

♥♥♥

The Guardian's Witch

England, 1290

Lord Alex Stelton can't resist a challenge, especially one with a prize like this: protect a castle on the Scottish border for a year, and it's his. Desperate for land of his own, he'll do anything to win the estate—even enter a proxy marriage to Lady Lisbeth Reynolds, the rumored witch who lives there.

Feared and scorned for her second sight, Lisbeth swore she'd never marry, but she is drawn to the handsome, confident Alex. She sees great love with him but fears what he would think of her gift and her visions of a traitor in their midst.

Despite his own vow never to fall in love, Alex can't get the alluring Lisbeth out of his mind and is driven to protect her when attacks begin on the border. But as her visions of danger intensify, Lisbeth knows it is she who must protect him. Realizing they'll secure their future only by facing the threat together, she must choose between keeping her magic a secret and losing the man she loves.

♥♥♥

Till Death Do Us Part

Lita Harris

Nikki and Nate's stable marriage is shattered when his law enforcement career is cut short by a stray bullet. Their future seems to be on the mend when Nikki inherits a family-run business in the woods of Maine.

Together they take ownership of the inn, but Nikki soon has doubts that her marriage will survive. The stress of hosting a wedding and remaining financially solvent threatens to ruin everything she's worked for. And concern for her young daughter—forced to leave New York City for the serene, laid-back country life—leaves Nikki unsure she made the right decision for her family. Will any of that matter when another change is thrown into the mix?

Dedicated to ~

Chocolate, and my fellow scribes who supply me with chocolate.

Till Death Do Us Part
by Lita Harris

A second wave of nausea threatened to take her out of commission. *Not today. Please.* Nikki struggled to lift her head without losing her breakfast on the lobby desk. This wedding was going to make or break their business and the stress got in the way of her normally organized hands-on manner.

Nate was doing the best he could to help with the preparations in spite of withdrawing from her even more. Ever since she'd mentioned she wanted a divorce, he'd stayed out of her way and acted like she'd never spoken the words. He didn't get that his increasing emotional distance is what made her spurt out those words to begin with. A moment of frustration and an argument over a wall plug outlet caused her to unleash words she wasn't sure she meant.

Balancing a business that was barely above water and imagining her life as a single mom weighed heavily on her. She'd gotten used to the dull ache in her head.

Thank God for Todd.

He came to her just in time to take on necessary repairs and help her out around the inn.

She cursed her grandmother as much as she loved her for leaving her the family headache.

"You okay, Mom?" Noelle lightly caressed her mom's brow.

Nikki moved with caution to keep from stirring her upset stomach more than it already was. "Would you get me a ginger ale, please?"

"Sure thing."

Her daughter, Noelle, was her world. *Such a good kid.* She seemed to be handling the disconnect between Nikki and Nate better than could be expected for a twelve-year-old girl.

Living in the seclusion of the Maine woods had a way of making an old soul out of someone so young.

Nikki knew that firsthand and saw the same growth in her daughter.

Noelle placed the can of soda in Nikki's hand. "Here you go. I took it from the wedding stock. Is that okay? I couldn't find any in the regular fridge."

She nodded. "Not a problem." But it was. They had been scraping by with the little bit of money to feed themselves. Before Nate lost his job they'd planned to only spend summers running the place. It was to be a second income and a place to get away and spend time as a family. She'd never anticipated it becoming their main source of income. The emergency fund was quickly eaten up by repairs and heating costs of two brutal Maine winters.

Nate did his best to come to terms with the fact that he couldn't stay on the police force. It wasn't his fault. The bullet came out of nowhere. One minute he was walking out of the coffee shop and the next thing he remembered was waking up in the back of an ambulance. His pension wasn't enough to keep their home in New York. The Loon Lake Inn had to be profitable to keep them going.

The ginger ale soothed her belly as she emptied the can. "So are we on track this morning?"

"Yep, Dad is raking the flower beds. Todd's working on the gazebo—he's almost done. It's looking pretty and almost new again."

"New as in that rustic Maine look?" She crushed the empty can and tossed it into the bin under the counter.

"Yes," Noelle giggled. "Weathered but sturdy. I'll drape the tulle when Todd's finished. I'm not putting out the daisies until Saturday before the ceremony."

Nikki smiled at the thought of daisies decorating the gazebo. It's the flower she would have chosen if she'd had the wedding of her dreams.

"Yeah, it's still too cold. I'm praying the weatherman is correct and it'll be a comfortable day. I've asked Todd to set up the portable gas heaters in case they're needed, so the guests are comfortable. You know how cool the nights can be. I want to make sure Viv and Gabe are happy with their wedding."

She touched her daughter's cheek. "I don't know what I'd do without you." The soulfulness of Noelle's eyes contradicted the youthful feel of her skin and perky disposition.

How did I create such a wonderful person?

Noelle's infectious smile had breathed joy into the past two years of Nikki's world. She'd watched Nate age from worry each day. The sparkle that danced in his eyes was replaced with sadness. At first she thought it was because of her. Was she getting too old? Was she not as much fun as she used to be? But damn it, she was fun to be around. Resentment festered in her even though she tried her best not to let it consume her.

The inn kept her busy and her mind off her marriage. This weekend was sure to throw enough her way and keep them at a safe distance, if only she could squash the headache and upset stomach.

"The next check-in isn't until later. Do you want to grab breakfast? It's Thursday—you know what that means: wild strawberry corn muffins." Nikki squeezed Noelle's hand, suggesting they head into the kitchen.

"Can't. I promised Agnes that I'd help her pick fiddleheads."

"For what? They're done for the season." She was all for encouraging guests to explore the woods but worried that Agnes might trip over something and get hurt.

"She wants to cook them for dinner."

"She's a guest, not a cook." Nikki wasn't about to let a guest into her kitchen. The last thing she needed was someone getting hurt.

"You tell her that. I don't mind. Plus, I like her stories."

"Enjoy yourself but keep an eye on her." Nikki worried that her daughter wasn't around kids her own age. It wasn't like Noelle could drop in at a friend's house like she used to when they'd lived in New York. Nikki was afraid that going from the big city to a remote environment would have a negative effect on Noelle during the teen years.

At least she didn't have to worry about strangers. Bears were what she feared most, though Noelle seemed fearless.

She left the lobby and went upstairs. Her nausea subsided; the soda helped. Her nerves were getting the better of her. Worrying about making the event profitable was a challenge to her financial skills. She hated numbers.

She hugged her knees to her chest on her bedroom window seat. Her head rested against the window as she hummed a song her mother used to when she hugged her as a scared child. She'd invited her mother to stay for the summer but she was away in England and had promised to visit for Christmas. *If* she could hold on to the inn that long.

They might be spending the holidays in the local shelter if they didn't catch a break soon.

Her low hum turned to song. "But will you dance with me under the cloud of love from long ago?"

She smiled as she remembered the song she wrote when she first met Nate. It wasn't about him, but he was the one who'd made her forget about the one that got away and broke her heart.

She glanced out the window and saw him bending over, scooping up the trash he'd raked out of the flower beds. Black-eyed Susans faced the sun and their bright yellow petals with dark brown centers always looked happy as the flowers swayed on their dainty stems. *Well, as happy as a flower can be.* She liked to think the feeling of life existed in all of creation. It gave her comfort and passion—something she'd been missing from her husband.

The disconnect was getting harder to fix, even though she still loved him. The distance was becoming too great to overcome.

She tried hard to remember his touch the way it used to be—the eagerness of his kiss, the happiness that once promised to carry them through forever until death did they part.

Their wedding day consisted of her sister, his best friend, and a mayor. They couldn't afford a big wedding and she'd convinced herself she was okay with that, but the truth was she missed not having a full-blown affair.

The flowers, music—she even missed having the poufy gown to trip over.

They'd hinted at getting married and one night got caught up in the romance of a spontaneous marriage. With her mother in England and Nate's parents away on a cruise to nowhere, Nikki and Nate went with it and settled on dinner at a small Italian restaurant that night. Garlic bread and pasta was all she had as a remembrance of her special day. Did she resent him? They had been in love and she'd convinced herself that it didn't matter. Being together was all she'd wanted.

She focused on the wail call of a loon on the lake. A walk through the trails was inviting, but she had to get things done. She looked down at Nate as sweat glistened on the nape of his neck and his white T-shirt plastered to his back, his ever-ready blue bandanna hanging from his jeans pocket. All she could see was the man she'd married and promised to love forever.

Could it be me? She wasn't any good at handling more than one disaster at a time. Maybe she was too demanding. The inn and the never-ending upkeep was getting in the way of her marriage. Maybe she was rash to ask for a divorce, but she couldn't think of any other way to get through to him.

She shook her hands as if shooing away an annoying gnat. "Gotta go. Gotta go." She rose from the window seat then paused by his side of the bed and smoothed out a wrinkle on his pillowcase.

Crash! She spun around toward the noise and ran to the hallway.

"Sorry, Nikki. I'm a clumsy sort." Albert stood over the shattered water pitcher.

She forced down the lump in her throat. "No worries. I've been meaning to move it forever." She hadn't—she loved the lightly faded and slightly cracked, now-demolished decoration. She'd picked it up on one of her yard sale hunts in an attempt to add her personal touch to the place.

Albert bent down to help. With his heavy breathing, she worried that he would pass out or worse. How would that look in the local paper? *Guest at The Loon Lake Inn Drops Dead Hours Before Wedding.*

"That's fine. I'll get it. It's no big deal." She scooped up the large pieces and kicked the smaller debris against the baseboard.

"I'm really sorry. I was looking for Agnes."

"She's walking the grounds with Noelle. Why don't you go look for her? I'm sure she wouldn't mind if you joined them." She forced a smile and went downstairs.

It was like having her grandparents underfoot, always wandering off and touching things. He followed her and she opened the door to let him out—free to look for his wife and away from any more fragile pieces. The grandfather clock chimed twelve.

Where'd the morning go? She hadn't thought she'd been upstairs so long. Her chest flushed and her breathing quickened. *Damn.*

Nate always complained how she waited to the last minute to get things done. The inn was about quiet and relaxation. *No more pity party of one.* She rushed downstairs. Enough stalling.

She slipped behind the lobby desk and Todd ran up to her waving his hands in the air.

"Eww, you reek. What did you fall into? You okay?" She backed away.

"There's a guest in my truck named Tara Graham whose car had a run-in with a bull."

She handed him a bottle of water and wished him away. He was stinking up the lobby. And she'd worked hard to get the inn ready for the wedding.

A few minutes later, a woman was escorted to the lobby desk by the bride-to-be.

"Another guest, Tara Graham." Viv smiled.

Nikki turned the guest book around and handed Tara a pen. "We like to make our guests feel welcome the minute they step foot in here." Even though she had computerized the reservation process, she liked the intimate feel of using the guest book. She thought it helped retain the rustic atmosphere of the place.

Tara was reluctant to take the pen.

"Of course, if you'd rather not…"

"No, that's okay." Tara hesitantly took the pen and scribbled an illegible signature. "I just had a horrible encounter with a moose. I'm still shaken."

Nikki suppressed a hearty laugh but it was hard not to smile. It wasn't unusual for people new to the area to be startled when coming in contact with an animal as large as a moose.

She smiled. "Todd told me about your incident."

"Yes. I'm just a bit shaken from the surroundings. I've never had so many trees around me."

"Hmm, city girl?"

"Yes, and my trip out here wasn't an easy one. She pushed back nonexistent glasses on top of her head.

Nikki checked the guest list in the computer. "You're early but your room is ready. I'll get someone to help you with your luggage."

"That won't be necessary. I don't have much."

"It's taken care of," Viv said from behind Tara.

"Enjoy your stay."

There was something familiar about Tara. Nikki did a quick computer search and found pictures of Tara plastered on the Internet. Award-winning musician. Possible love triangle? No wonder Tara was so frazzled. "Well, the paparazzi definitely won't find her here." Nikki laughed.

♥♥♥

"The gazebo is just about done. Wanna check it? The only thing needed is the light, which is coming tomorrow," Todd called in through the lobby window.

"Be right there." She grabbed a cracker. Her stomach was churning again, not enough to cause her discomfort but enough to be annoying.

She stepped out onto the open front porch. The rocking chair Todd had made was inviting but she was running out of time. Maybe later she could convince Nate to spend some time with her as the sun set. She smiled remembering back to the first night they took over as the new owners. When they'd made plans to make a life for themselves in the woods of Maine, away from the city. She'd convinced herself they could adapt to the country life. After all, she was familiar with the area and embraced the serenity of the woods. Having spent most summers there, it was like her second home. And she vowed to make the adjustment a seamless one for the family. Like she'd done many times in their marriage whenever the status quo was threatened, it was her who took care of making the impossible work. Nate wasn't comfortable with change. No wonder he was content with the state of their marriage—she took care of everything and it was exhausting keeping his life carefree. This time was a challenge and she was tired but she wanted to pull it together.

Wooden barrels of yellow-and-purple wildflowers cuddled with Queen Anne's lace lined the porch stairs and walkway. Nate had done a fantastic job raking up debris, which was a difficult feat considering the never-ending onslaught of tree litter and whatever paper, empty nutshells, or some other foreign items the animals decided to drag across the gravel walkway.

She stopped short of the gazebo and took in the structure and its surroundings. It was the perfect wedding setup. Todd had managed to age the new wood so it blended in with the old.

The rough Maine winters certainly took their toll on things.

She could picture the white tulle flowing along the outline of the canopy, adorned with white daisies and the sun's rays beaming down, isolating the ceremonial area. She made a note to tell Noelle to hold off draping the material until Saturday. Today was too early to risk ruining the delicate fabric. Even though she liked to get things done early, it was better to wait this time.

"This looks wonderful. Thank you for taking care of this. I know carpentry wasn't what you signed on for."

Todd gathered up his hammer, handsaw, and nails. "No problem. I didn't have any nature walks planned. Nothing until tomorrow morning."

"Well, thanks anyway." Nikki smiled and walked away. She could never spend too much time alone around Todd. He excited her in a way that made her feel sensual, and it was wrong. The knot in her stomach weighed heavily whenever he smiled at her. At times, she thought he'd paid more attention to her than just an employee. Nothing out of line, but she definitely sensed a connection. She thought she was attracted to him because he gave her the attention her husband didn't. Either way, she didn't want to come across as interested. She wasn't about to exchange one complication for another.

She rambled off to a narrow path behind the gazebo. She looked back to make sure Todd wasn't behind her. The sunlight faded as pine trees surrounded her and the gravel beneath her feet changed to dirt. *Damn. Should have changed my shoes.*

She hadn't intended to wander off and her wedge sandals weren't the best foot protection. A broken tree branch offered a place to rest. She rested her hand on her grumbling stomach, no longer nauseous but famished. *I just ate. No, can't be.*

One, two…she counted off on her fingers.

She closed her eyes and took a deep breath. Her shoulders fell with a heavy sigh. *Impossible.* One more thing to complicate her life.

A spruce grouse ran between her feet and startled her as she stood and the log heaved a bit. Brush rustled behind her. She held her breath. Holly branches moved. *Bear?* She released her breath slowly—the last thing she wanted to do was spook a wild animal. It sounded too subtle to be a moose. *Please don't let it be a momma moose with calves.* She was still and waited for evidence of what stalked her. *Please, please, please.*

It came closer and every muscle in her body seized. *I know I'm not religious, but…*

"Nikki. Why are you out here all alone?" Agnes held on to a wicker basket filled with…well, she couldn't make it out, but it could be anything. Someone's car keys, beer cans, something someone threw away. The woods were filled with lost objects.

"Just checking the grounds." She laughed at her silliness thinking it was a bear.

"Agnes, where are you?" Noelle yelled from the brush.

"We're over by the abandoned trail," Nikki yelled back. Gratitude filled her chest as the thought of being devoured by a bear left her. "We'll meet you by the trailhead."

She took hold of Agnes's elbow and marched her out of the woods. Cars filled the parking area. Noelle caught up with them and shook her finger at Agnes. "I swear, if you take off on me like that again, I'll never go fiddlehead hunting with you, especially if they're in season."

"Sorry, dear," Agnes said.

"You scared me to death. Uh, Mom. Who's watching the desk?" Noelle ran to the front porch.

That's it. Pull yourself together. "Come on. You're staying with me until your husband comes for you. I can't have you wandering off in the woods while I have to work."

She lovingly took the basket from Agnes and they strolled to the inn. She knew Noelle would handle any situation presented at the desk. She couldn't figure out where her daughter inherited her instinct for problem solving but appreciated that she could help out.

"Oh—" She caught her breath as they walked into the lobby to find Nate behind the desk. He was talking to Albert and cut the conversation short when he looked up and saw Nikki.

"I've been looking for you. Can we talk?" He motioned for Noelle to man the reception desk.

♥♥♥

Nate slipped his hand into hers and they strolled along the river rock path toward the duck pond. His touch felt foreign and distant to her, like they barely knew each other.

She pulled back "I really need…"

"Just give me some of your time." He let go of her and slid his hands into his front jeans pockets.

"But I need to get back. There's a lot going on today." She wasn't in the mood for an intense discussion and stepped back to leave.

"I'm taking a job." He didn't even turn around, just stared across the pond.

"You have a job." If his goal was to get her attention, he succeeded.

"No, you have a job. This is yours. I seriously thought I could make a go of this but all it's seemed to do is create another obstacle in our relationship."

She couldn't argue with him—she was all too aware of the wedge that kept widening the gap in their marriage. Even with that, he couldn't up and leave. She remembered the night they found out he couldn't return to work. Oh, he was offered a desk job, but that wouldn't keep him happy. He tried it for a month and nearly crawled up the wall. No, he needed something that kept him moving and not confined to one spot all day. Together they'd thought that taking over the inn would give them the opportunity to be financially independent. They could pursue what made them happy. She could stay home and pick up her music again—she'd been away from it for too long and missed it. Nate would have the freedom to do whatever he wanted. Build things to keep his hands busy until he decided on something concrete. Noelle would have a safe place to grow up and be able to go outside without them having to worry about her whereabouts.

He turned to her, his hands digging deeper into his pockets. "Face it, Nikki. This isn't working. I've tried to talk to you about it but you're always lost in your own head."

"I never meant to ignore you, it's just…"

"Too easy." He laughed. "I thought it was a blessing when you inherited this place. It was familiar. It came at a time when we needed it. I get it, but it's not working for me." He picked up a rock and skipped it across the pond.

The next one made it all the way across. "Maybe this job offer came at a good time. It'll give us time apart and give you time to see if you really want a divorce."

She pulled back her shoulders and caught her breath. *Damn.* This was the first time he acknowledged her mention of ending their marriage. It had an entirely different sound to it when he said it. Doubt inched to the surface and she questioned her decision.

"Where's the job?"

He hesitated. "California."

Her chest tightened at the idea of him moving across the country. How could he up and leave their daughter? A divorce or separation was one thing, but moving three thousand miles was—

She grabbed a rock, ran her finger hard along the ragged edge, and lobbed it across the water.

"So you think that's the answer? You're miserable. Don't you think that Noelle and I feel it? Don't you think your mood infects the atmosphere of the house?" She picked up a larger stone but this time skimmed it with such force that it hardly broke the surface as it skipped away from her.

"Do you ever stop to think what I'm going through?" He lowered his voice to a tone she was more receptive to.

Nate had become too comfortable with snapping at her and she cringed every time he did it. She missed how she used to smile when he spoke. *Maybe it's me.* She willed a wave of calm through her being. *Breathe. Breathe.* She released her breath as tension left her body. She'd give him a chance to have his say, even though it was hard for her to wait out his long-winded conversations.

"Fine. Talk." She sighed.

"Can you at least pretend to be concerned?"

"Sorry. Just stressed over the wedding details." She

hoped the bride and groom wouldn't be faced with the end of their marriage at some point in their lives.

He put his hands on her shoulders. She looked him straight in the eye.

"I get that, and I know this isn't the best time to have this conversation, but you're impossible to get to stay in one place…"

"Just busy." She clenched her fists.

"I know that. I'm not undermining what you're doing here, but this isn't working the way we planned. I need something more to do. This isn't cutting it for me. I don't feel productive living like this. Do you understand that?" He shook her shoulders then let go.

Nikki relaxed her fingers and stepped back. Her eyes welled up. "I know it's not." She swiped away a tear. "Nothing about this is going right. The only one who's okay with it is Noelle, and honestly I'm not a hundred percent sure about that. I'm sure she misses her friends and the malls, but she doesn't complain."

"She always did seem smarter than us." He grinned. She smiled. He was trying to lighten the situation that was beyond them.

"I don't want to rush you, but can we get to the point?"

"Todd told me about a place he used to work for and gave me a contact and it turns out that I know the guy." He dug his toe in the dirt and looked away from her. He could never look her in the eye when he expected her to lash out.

"Todd, huh?"

"Yep."

"What's the job?"

"Communication security."

"What the hell does that mean?"

"It's a company that monitors telecommunications."

"What does that have to do with you?" Her eyes narrowed. "Is this a real job or are you looking for a reason to leave?"

He straightened his back. "Isn't that what you wanted?"

Why did this have to happen now? He spent days avoiding her, even though he blamed her because she was the one who said she wanted the divorce. Typical Nate. Totally oblivious to his shortcomings but he sure remembered hers. "You know what? The only thing I want right now is to get this event going and over with."

She turned her back to him.

"They want me there Monday."

She folded her arms across her chest and dug her nails into her skin to quell the anger rising in her throat, and walked away.

She stopped with her back to him. "I have a question for you."

"Go ahead." She sensed he was still standing where she'd left him.

"Do you want a divorce?" Her tone was softer, but stern.

"I never said I did." The sound of leaves being crushed faded as he walked back into the woods.

♥♥♥

Nikki hadn't intentionally ignored Nate since they'd spoke about his leaving the day before. Damn elevator crapped out and the last thing she'd needed was for that to not be working. It being the day before the wedding and night of the pre-ceremony, she had to step it up to get things done. Todd was quick to fix it and had Nate help him so that kept him busy that morning.

"Mom." Noelle dropped a wicker basket of linens on the kitchen floor. "Do you want these set out now?"

She tossed the dish towel on the counter, grateful for some conversation. Sometimes she got so deep into her thoughts that she lost track of time. "You've been doing so much. Why don't you take a break?"

"Agnes offered to set up the tables. I just want to know if you want it done now."

"But she's a…oh, never mind. Let her do it if she wants to. She'll just get in the way if you don't let her."

"Yep, that's what I thought." Noelle pulled out a chair.

"I might have to put her on the payroll." She smiled at her attempt to provide some levity to her mood. She picked up the basket and put it on the kitchen table. "These can be put out later today. No sense having them in the way and get dirty. There's too many people in and out of the room."

"Mom, you're babbling." Noelle took a seat at the table and grabbed a banana. "You know, Mom…" She waved the fruit to drive home her point. "You and Dad babble when things are bothering you. Well, you babble. He uses more words than necessary but doesn't say much."

"And you don't talk like a normal twelve-year-old. You spend too much time around adults." She peeled a banana and joined her daughter. She loved spending time with her and this summer had been extra special. Noelle spent more time around the house, which Nikki enjoyed, but she also worried that her sweet little girl was becoming a hermit and missing out on developing her own age-appropriate support system. Noelle never spoke of friends or brought any home.

"Blame the Internet. I'm simply exposed to too much."

"I'll have to ground you from the computer."

"Sure, once I show you how to use it." Noelle rolled her eyes.

She sat back with arms folded and looked closely at her daughter. She'd been so caught up in her own head that she didn't even consider how a divorce would affect the child they created. Was she really done with her marriage or reacting to the financial stress?

Damn. Why had she quit smoking? She could go for a cigarette right now.

She glanced at the clock over the sink. It was too early for a brandy—plus, she liked to think that her daughter didn't know that she had an occasional drink. Did Noelle know about Nate's job? No, she couldn't. He wouldn't be that careless to say something about a major life change to their daughter without her being there.

"Dad's been weird lately." She ran her hands down her ponytail, something she did when she needed to confide in her mother.

"How so?" She had to play dumb to find out what Noelle suspected.

"I mean weirder than when we first moved here. At first he was a little excited about being here. Now, he never smiles. I see him walking around like he's confused. What's his problem? He hardly speaks to me anymore." Noelle picked at the seedless grapes in the ceramic strainer that had unintentionally become the table centerpiece. Nikki had developed a penchant for scouring local yard sales as a means of social interaction and bought the chipped colander to be nice, never intending it to take up permanent residency and become the focal point of her kitchen.

She walked behind Noelle and hugged her. "I know, sweetie, it's been tough for him. He thought he would retire from the police force. Getting shot changed our lives in ways that we couldn't imagine."

"I know. The shooting didn't only affect him." Noelle tightened the grip on her hair as she finger-combed her tresses.

The pit of her stomach ached—her innocent child was more aware of the issues than she'd thought. She wanted to scoop up her daughter and make everything better. If they could get through this weekend and deal with each crisis after the wedding was over... That's all she needed—time.

"Do you know where your dad is now?"

"He was still with Todd."

"Elevator's not done?"

"They seemed to be finishing up."

Nikki held Noelle's chin in her hand. "Answer me honestly. I know we kind of jumped into this adventure. You know, leaving the wilds of the city for the tame wilderness of country life. What's your feelings about living here?"

"Mom, there are bears here."

"Little ones. My question is, do you like it here?"

Nikki patiently waited for the response.

"I do like it here. I mean, it's not the city. I can't do very much on my own, but the city doesn't have trees. I like hearing the birds in the morning. So I do like that part of being here. I miss the city, too."

"You're rambling and being evasive like your father." She grinned.

"Sorry, I got the worst traits of both of you. Not my fault." Noelle blew Nikki a kiss.

"Okay, maybe if I put it this way: If you had a choice, would you stay here or go back to the city?"

Noelle stood up and whisked the basket off the table. "I would choose whatever place kept you and Dad together." She left the kitchen as Nikki stood in awe, as if she'd been kicked in the stomach. *Damn kid is too smart for me.*

She went to the sink and slammed the faucet on full blast. How could she have been so stupid to think Noelle wouldn't figure out something was wrong? *Grown-ups acting like kids. The kid acting like the grown-up.*

A male scarlet tanager flew up to the window and hovered for a few seconds. Unusual for one of them to come so close to the house. All the summers she'd spent in the Maine woods, she'd never seen the elusive bird— only heard the stories that if you were lucky enough to see one, make a wish real fast. She crunched her eyes and wrinkled her nose. Her hope was unleashed into the universe. But she couldn't tell anyone what she wished because it might not come true if she did. A tingle ran down her spine. She took that as a sign and hummed as she relaxed, washed the last dish, and wiped her hands thoroughly, as if wiping away her troubles.

♥♥♥

The kitchen tasks were behind her. Maybe she had been too hard on Nate. She went in search of him and wandered down the hall. Music flowed into the open air. *Pretty.* It brought her back to her time in college as a music major when she was going to write at least five award-winning songs. That dream was squashed when she fell in love with Nate. It was her own fault—like with everything else, she put herself last. He was in the police academy and they'd needed to pay the rent. So she packed away her notebook. The memory of selling her piano— sure she'd be able to buy a newer and better one— brought tears to her eyes. Her plans rarely worked out and this dream was no exception. The universe always seemed to have a different path for her to take.

Stop it. Pull yourself together. She willed herself to purge the thought of failure from her mind, opting to follow the music instead.

She came upon Tara sitting on the bench, her shoulders hunched over the keys as she played the piano, immersed in her song. It was a posture she herself held many times as she struggled to find the right key for the melody forming in her head.

Not wanting to break the creation in progress, she waited in the doorway until Tara raised her head and stopped playing.

"That's very pretty. Are you playing it for the wedding?" She pulled up a chair next to Tara at the piano bench.

"Possibly. I've been tossing around a few bars in my head and wanted to test out the melody. Thought I'd take advantage of the room being empty. The acoustics are terrific in here." Tara gave her full attention to Nikki. "Do you play?"

"A little. I know that's not the best piano but it came with the inn and it seemed to fit the room, so we kept it." Occasionally, she'd tap the keys when dusting but never sat down to play because she didn't want to know if her talent had faded. "Would you play some more?"

"Sure, but please take a seat next to me." Tara patted the space next to her on the bench.

She was happy to be seated at the piano for the first time in years.

"Show me what you got." Tara sat up straight and away from the keyboard. She folded her arms casually across her chest.

Nikki froze. *I can't do this.* It was as if Tara silently dared her to play. Nikki's hands wavered over the keyboard. The black and white keys were tempting, but what if she sucked? She flexed her fingers and paused. She closed her eyes and drew in a soft breath, hoping that Tara didn't notice her hesitance. She lowered her left hand and tapped a key with her thumb. The rest of her hand followed suit and she was committed. Excitement surged through her fingertips, up her arms, and into her heart. She struck a chord and it sounded right, it was where she wanted it to be. She opened her eyes and struck the next chord and winced from the awful sound. She adjusted her hands and closed her eyes again, letting her fingers go where they wanted to.

But will you dance with me under the cloud from love long ago?

She hummed softly as her fingers glided over the keys, her confidence getting stronger with each correct tap of the key.

"That's beautiful," Tara assured her.

Nikki froze and pulled back her hands. "I'm very rusty. It's nothing." She slid her hands down her thighs. A twinge of bravado let her know she was a fool for letting her dream fall by the wayside. She couldn't blame Nate for this—it was all her. He never would have told her to quit; she did it to herself.

"I've never heard that piece. Where did you get it from?"

She hesitated. This was her chance to introduce her music to someone who mattered. After all, she was sitting with an award-winning musician who wanted to know about her. Would she come across as a wannabe songwriter who would never be better than a teenager plinking at the piano keys, who wrote songs about her boyfriend leaving her for her best friend? She could be embarrassed, suck it up, and move on. Or be honest and maybe find a way to permanently reconnect to her passion.

"Seriously, I think it's good. I'd like to hear more."

Her stomach fluttered and she felt herself blushing. "There isn't any more. I wanted to be a songwriter but my life took a different direction." Nikki sat back and crossed her legs, ensuring she wouldn't continue to play.

"What happened?"

"Life." She rolled her eyes. It was easy to blame her procrastinating on something else.

"I realize that, but if you're meant to write then it's there. The great thing about being a writer and musician is you can do it anywhere. I know." Tara tilted her head back and laughed. "One of my best songs was written in a ladies' room stall while I was snowed in at an airport."

"Some of what I felt were my best melodies came to me while I was in the shower." Nikki smiled. Her stomach was doing flip-flops and her mood lifted talking about music to someone who got it.

"See what I mean? No one has to know where your inspiration came from. But you do have to put it out there. Be it words, music, or both, you have to get it out there, otherwise you'll strangle yourself from the inside." Tara made a twisting motion with her fist.

It was like a lightning bolt surged through her. Tara was right. That was exactly how Nikki felt. She wanted to get back to her notebook. Words swirled around her head and she needed to write them down before she forgot them. But she had to get back to work—at least for now until the weekend was over. Well, maybe she could steal a few minutes.

"I'll let you get back to what you need to do. Thank you for letting me sit with you." She stood to leave.

"Anytime. It was nice to watch you play your piece. Maybe you can finish it while I'm here and I'll get to listen to all of it." Tara winked at Nikki.

She left the room, closed the door behind her, and let out a huge smile as she ran upstairs to her bedroom.

♥♥♥

Nikki flung open the door, ready to grab her paper and pen. She wanted to write—get the melody out of her head and onto something tangible. She yanked open the nightstand drawer and the contents sprung out like a jack-in-the-box. Her hands rummaged through old tissue, erasers, marbles, and outdated pocket calendars. "Ah." A half-filled steno pad was at the bottom of the drawer with a pen clipped to the cover. "Hello, my old friend."

She climbed onto the bed and fluffed the pillows to support her back. Curling up on her bed had been her favorite writing position; maybe it would still work for her. With her legs folded under her thighs, pillows in position, and creative desire unleashed, she whipped open the notebook and clicked the pen—and stared at the blank page. "Agh!"

The dreaded white sheet of terror.

She tapped the pen on the page. Her excitement was waning. *No…no.* She steadied herself and promised she'd get serious about her rekindled passion.

This wasn't going to work no matter how badly she wanted to get going. She lay back with her head on the pillows and plopped the notebook over her face. With her eyes closed and the scent of paper filling her nostrils, she hummed the melody wreaking havoc in her head. *Come on. I need it on paper.*

"Oh, sorry. Didn't know you were here."

Her body lurched when Nate entered the room.

"I'll leave you be." His voice was kinder than it was the last time they spoke.

"No, that's okay." She pulled the notebook off her face, thinking it would be nicer to talk to him without it blocking her vision. "Just taking a break."

He walked toward her. "I came up here to hide myself. I checked in a few people."

She shot up. "Crap. I should be down there."

"Relax. Noelle is taking care of the desk."

"I really should be available in case someone needs something." She stood up and stuffed the shuffled contents back into the drawer but held on to her notebook.

"Everything's fine. Noelle knows where to find you. Plus, Todd is talking to people about his nature walks." He walked closer to her.

She stiffened her back and the excitement she felt about her song slipped away as the realization of her life crept into focus.

"Can we talk?" He sat on the bed.

"I can't." She started to walk past him. Why did he always want to talk when she wasn't in the mood or couldn't?

He grabbed her arm. "Please. You haven't said a word since I told you about the job."

"What is there to discuss? You've made up your mind and without talking to me first. It never used to be like that." She pulled her arm from his grasp.

"You're right, and we also never had money issues," he sniped back at her. He took a breath and relaxed his stance. He stared at her. "I hate what's happened to us."

She hung her head. "I know," she whispered. "That's not true about the money issues. Remember when you where in the academy? I quit everything to get us through that financially." He hated when she threw that in his face but it was true.

"Why does that still eat away at you? I begged you how many times to get back to your music once I got out of the academy. You can't hold that against me." He stepped closer. "I never once asked you to give up anything. Never."

Her lips tightened. She clenched the notebook. "You didn't have to ask. What were we going to do? Your career, then Noelle came—I didn't have any support system."

He reached out to her.

She stood back. "Just so you know, I'm not happy with the way things turned out. I honestly thought taking on this business would put us in a better place. I mean, do you know how hard it is to deal with you? Ever since your accident, I've done everything I could to make our life better. Do you think I don't know what it's like for your career to have ended prematurely? That I don't know what it's like to have your dreams squashed through no fault of your own?"

She wanted to cry. She wanted to run out of the room and have a total meltdown. She *needed* to have a meltdown. That was the only way she was able to regain her footing when things got bad. But she'd become so hardened that she wouldn't allow herself to fall apart even to rebuild, no matter how necessary it was.

"And that, sweetheart, is where I think you're wrong. I didn't see the bullet coming. I didn't have any control over the damage it did to my body—that it forced me to leave the department. You, on the other hand, have always had the power to sit at a piano and pick up your career that you so conveniently abandoned, though you blame me." His eyes seared into her. "Do you think that I don't hear you humming that same tune over and over? Whatever it is, finish it and stop blaming me. I may have caused other issues in our marriage, but not that one."

The pen dug into her wrist as she clenched her fists. She could see the frustration in his eyes. The hurt in his heart. "I have to go." She walked past him and he grabbed her from behind and spun her around.

"Knock it off with this martyr crap. When did this become who you are?" He yanked the notebook from her clutches. "Is this what it's all about?"

She didn't answer him. She pulled on her arm to get away.

"I'm not leaving before I know if it's me or your discarded dreams that are making you miserable." He tightened his grip on her upper arms and pulled her into him. His lips came to her with a force she'd never experienced. Her shoulders softened and the pen she held so tightly fell to the floor.

She couldn't fight him—she didn't want to.

His lips made her feel like she was being carried away on a cloud. She slid her arm around his neck and pulled him in closer. His musky scent awakened her desire for him and the vise she had encased her heart in began to weaken.

He loosened his hold on her. "Think about what's really bothering you." He placed the notebook back in her hand and left the room.

♥♥♥

The powerful touch of his hands on her arms lingered for hours. His kiss still on her lips. She couldn't focus the rest of the day. Fortunately, the event was running smoothly. She hadn't expected Viv and Gabe to bring a wedding planner, who really wasn't but turned out to be a family member who liked to coordinate weddings.

She'd been thinking of ways to make the business work and maybe weddings weren't the way to go. *He can't leave.* If they had a different strategy it could change their course. It was best to get through the next two days and then sort out their future—whatever that would be.

She put her notebook on the bench, sat down at the piano, and plunked the keys. *He was right.* It was her that got in her own way. When had she become so judgmental? So cold and uncaring? She didn't mean to be. *Plunk. Plunk. Plink.* It would take practice if she wanted to succeed. In her songwriting career and marriage. At least she had the parent thing right; her daughter would have told her if she hadn't.

Maybe the wilds of Maine were too remote for a year-round residence, but she didn't see any other way. Everything they had was tied up in this place and she was tired of thinking about it.

She opened her notebook flat on top of the baby grand and scanned the words. *But will you dance…* "No, that sucks." *Plink, plink.* "Hmm, something else." She crossed out the first line. "Will you stay with me as the tides change? Will you love me as the years go by? Will you stay forever? Agh!" She threw the pen on the notebook. The words weren't coming to her.

"I don't have it anymore. Maybe I never did." She spun on the bench and flinched seeing Tara beside her.

"I knew you were aching to get something out." Tara smiled.

"I've been fooling myself." She put her head down on the keys, unleashing a serious discord.

"I've never seen anyone play that way, but hey, maybe you're on to something."

"It should be easier. It used to be." She lifted her head and propped it against her palm.

Tara sat down next to her. "You're right, but if it was that easy, anyone could do it. It's like anything. It takes work and practice."

"But it seems to come so naturally to you." And that

wasn't happening. She was compelled to get the song written before the wedding. She wanted Tara's opinion of her finished piece. She *was* looking for approval.

"It does, but not always, and if I stay away from it for too long I get rusty, like you said earlier. That's all it is. If you weren't a writer you wouldn't be obsessing over not being able to." Tara stood up to leave. "It sounds to me like you're clogged up. You need to do something to get that energy moving again."

"Too busy." Nikki closed her notebook and clipped the pen to the front cover. But she was lying to herself— she wasn't busy. It was her way of keeping herself from thinking too much. And she hadn't even been good at that lately.

"That's a convenient excuse, isn't it? And how long has it been working for you? A few years at least? When do you think you'll have the time? Next decade?" Tara crossed her arms like she was scolding a lazy student.

"Do you talk to all of your acquaintances like you're their teacher?" Nikki laughed.

"No, just the people I feel are stuck but serious about writing. It's the same speech my mentor gave to me. Comes in handy when I feel the need to hole up and forget about everything."

Nikki stood up and held her notebook against her chest. "Thanks. See you tomorrow at the wedding. Enjoy the party tonight."

She left the room. Tara was right. It was too easy to push aside what she feared, starting with the failure of her marriage. She walked past a flurry of activity in the lobby. She sneaked past Drew, the local sheriff, and some girl she didn't know.

She slipped into the kitchen and out the back door. Fresh air filled her lungs and the sweet aroma of the rose hedge satisfied her need to get outside. All she wanted was a quick walk by herself to clear her head. People traipsed about the grounds. *Why did I worry so much?* From a quick assessment, it appeared that things were falling into place.

She sat on a log swing for two that her grandfather had made and hung from the century old willow tree on the property. No one was sure how old the tree was but they took her grandfather at his word. She stabbed her toes in the dirt and set the swing in motion. The gentle sway fed her senses and she spread her notebook open on her lap. It brought her back to her younger years when she'd met Nate and the first time she'd brought him to the inn. Being a city kid, he wasn't too keen on being in the woods. He would jump at the slightest sound, thinking it was a bear. Even the chirps of crickets bothered him and he could never sleep well when he was there. She should've known moving here wouldn't be a good idea.

It was you. It was Nate; she knew that now.

"That's it." She pounded the paper with the tip of the pen and her heart quickened.

It was you who made me see.
The beginning of a new me.
I didn't know back then that it would never end.
I only wanted to love you and have you next to me.
You showed me what I never knew.
And that was to spend my life with you.

Her grip tightened around the pen and she held the notebook against her chest. A smile as wide as she could muster hurt her cheeks, but she had it. The melody in her head was Tara's but the words were hers. A crack rippled within her and a rush of air filled her chest. Confidence took her over. This one she was going to finish.

♥♥♥

Spilled alcohol was mopped up. Flattened cheddar cheese cubes were scraped from the floor, and the occasional broken glass was swept away. Things would be clean and quiet again once the wedding was over.

Nikki had hardly spoken to Nate—not that she didn't want to, just no time. He'd been up checking in guests and she went to bed early. She was more tired than usual and had nagging nausea earlier that morning. It would all be over in a few hours.

She poured a glass of ginger ale from behind the bar and rested against her hands on the counter, rolling the glass with her palms. *Oh no.* She looked at the calendar underneath the shelf. *No! Can't be.*

She abandoned her soda and ran upstairs to her bedroom. She tore into her closet, digging through plastic bags stuffed on the shelf. She grabbed the opened box and went into the master bathroom. She took a deep breath and peed on the test stick. *Can't be. Not now.* She held her forehead and waited out the required three minutes. A hint of result filled the window. *Two more minutes to be sure.* She put the test on the sink and pulled herself together counting off the minutes in her head.

Earlier that year she was late but it turned out to be nothing. She washed her face and held the towel against her wet skin. She peeked past the edge of the towel with one eye and glanced at the tiny window that had the power to change the course of her life yet again.

Positive.

"Damn it." She sat on the edge of the tub and held her belly. "Why now?"

It wasn't that she didn't want another child. She loved children, but it had been difficult to conceive again.

She felt bad that Noelle didn't have a sibling, but that was the way things worked out. Until now.

She slipped the result stick into a small plastic bag, shoved it into her back pocket, and ambled to her bed. She sat with a thud and her mind began to spin, but she didn't have time for a pity party, not with a wedding going on. Sweat beaded on her palms. She rubbed them against her jeans. Maybe it's a bad test stick. *Sigh.* Her notebook called to her so she flipped to the song she'd started. The words felt right.

Here we are years later with a deeper desire.
But can't find our way back through the fire.
As many doors opened, more closed behind us.
Dreams shattered, hope faded, it was all a bust.
I sit here searching for an answer.
No more hurt, a gentle hint of closure.
We've been through so much.
All I want is to feel your touch.
To find our way back to the past.
Whatever the future may cast.

She smiled and was happy with the words she wrote—that was good enough for now. The words that were bottled up, choking her, were finally out in the open. A wave of relief spread over her and for the first time in months she felt clear. She tossed her pad on the bed and went downstairs.

The kitchen was bustling with pre-wedding activity. Trays of stuffed mushrooms waited to be baked at the last minute. Chocolate mousse filled the refrigerator. She made a mental note to hold one back for herself. She walked along the counters checking off the food to make sure everything was accounted for and the timing was on schedule. She was glad the bride and groom opted for a buffet; it made things mush easier.

"How are you feeling?"

She almost jumped out of her skin. She hated when Nate snuck up on her.

"Fine. Why do you ask?" Did she look pregnant already? She turned to face him and felt for her back pocket. Was the proof sticking out?

"You went to bed earlier than you usually do."

"True, but then I got up to check in some last-minute guests. The interruption threw me off. That's all."

"Where have you been?" She cupped his elbow and moved them out of the way. The ceremony was in a few minutes and the frenzy was getting in the way of their conversation—plus, the smell of the shrimp cocktail on the sideboard made her queasy.

"Helping Todd with the lawn chairs. We're ready when they are."

"I need to…"

"It's time!" Agnes scurried through the kitchen, rounding up anyone who would listen. "Come on." She yanked Nikki's arm and pulled her outside.

Nate followed them.

Tara took her seat at the rented piano. Nikki wouldn't dare move the baby grand from the banquet room. It was too big and old to move around.

The sun rested on the horizon. A soft wind flowed across the lawn, just enough to be cool. Tulle cascaded along the outline of the gazebo.

"Noelle did a beautiful job with that, didn't she?" Nikki smiled. She was so proud of her daughter. Would there be another? She looked at Nate. Her news was going to change their plans and she hoped he'd be happy with another child. Maybe it wouldn't change the outcome of their marriage, but it would affect them as parents having two kids to worry about.

The final guest sat down and Tara played the first note. The bridal party walked down the aisle, dropping rose petals along the way. Nikki immediately recognized the music. It was the same melody Tara played when she was practicing.

Gabe and his groomsmen lined up to the right of the gazebo. Nikki leaned down to check under the tulle. Yep, Todd put the light up in time. She knew she could count on him—he was always a step ahead of her.

Viv appeared at the end of the aisle in her beautiful yet understated gown.

Nikki thought back to her wedding. Nate was full of life. He'd found fun in everything he did.

Not so much now. How would their lives change once she told him her news? She caught her breath.

It could shut him down completely, or—

The music grew louder.

"It was you who made me see,
"The beginning of a new me.
"I didn't know back then that it would never end."

Nikki gasped and put her hand over her mouth. "That's…"

"Your song." Nate gently squeezed her side.

Tara's music. Her words. She clasped her mouth and tears rimmed her eyes as her insides trembled.

Tara continued.

"I only wanted to love you and have you next to me.
"You showed me what I never knew.
"And that was to spend my life with you."

The music softened as Viv met Gabe to begin their life as a married couple.

She mouthed a *Thank you* to Tara. Nate pulled her in closer. Was he crying? She thought his eyes were glistening with tears.

"Thank you." She reached up to kiss him but hesitated. She was confused. What if he really wanted to leave? Maybe it was her hormones making her crazy.

"I now pronounce you husband and wife." The minister spoke and the newly married couple, followed by their bridal party, walked into the reception room with the guests close behind.

Nate walked Nikki onto the dance floor and held her tight. She never needed the big wedding, after all. It wasn't the cost or abundance of flowers and food that made the marriage. It was the couple—and they had that when they married.

♥♥♥

The night was flawless. The sunset timed perfectly and the weather was the most beautiful Maine night Nikki had ever experienced. The party was in full swing and they could relax.

Nate hadn't left her side all night, but they had been too distracted to talk.

"It looks like we can steal away now. There's enough alcohol to keep people happy and the dinner is over." Nate held her hand and she welcomed his touch.

"Yep, nothing but a party now." She had to tell him. She wasn't sure if her stomach was churning from hunger, being pregnant, or the fact that she hadn't told him yet. "Come on."

She walked with him into the empty kitchen and pulled out a chocolate mousse from the fridge. He handed her a spoon.

"I'm surprised that lasted so long." He laughed.

"Chocolate never lasts very long around me." She took a spoonful and swallowed hard. "Sit down."

"I'll pass out if I do. I'm exhausted."

She pulled out a chair for him.

"Please. You're going to need to be as close to the floor as possible so you don't get hurt if you pass out." She put down the dessert cup.

"Is there any more mousse?" He picked up her empty container and scooped out what little bit was left with his finger.

"Um, there could be but, uh, not now." She did have one hidden but was saving it for herself in case he had a bad reaction to her news.

"This might change things." She pulled out the test stick and held it up for him to see.

His eyes widened. "You're pregnant?"

She nodded. "Guilty."

"I can't believe that. After all these years of trying, you're—"

"Yes, pregnant." She studied his face. Well? He was shocked, but beyond that she wasn't sure. She measured her words. "Of course this would happen when we plan on getting a divorce and you're moving cross country."

He hung his head. "Well, part of that isn't true."

"What do you mean?"

"The job fell through. I found out this morning. Turns out the company was bought out and they're not filling any new in-house positions at this time."

She was relieved; one less problem to worry about—at least for now. "They didn't know that when they offered you the job?" She exchanged the stick for the dessert cup.

"Apparently not the person who hired me. But even though that position fell through, they did offer me another one. It's a telecommuting job. I can work from home ninety-five percent of the time. You're pregnant?"

"Seems so." She licked her chocolate-mousse-covered spoon like a lollipop. "What about the other five percent?"

"That would require traveling. But it's only five percent of the time."

He shook his head and stood up. "You're really pregnant?"

"According to the test."

He steadied himself, legs spread like they were planted in the ground and arms crossed. That all-important stance when he was serious and nobody took him seriously. "So that leaves…?"

She grabbed two dishes of chocolate mousse from the refrigerator. "The last of the dessert."

She knew him well enough to know he was excited about the pregnancy, but with the possibility of divorce still hanging over them, his cautious nature held his excitement at bay.

"Us." She ate a spoonful of mousse.

"Ah, yeah. You're the one who wants the divorce." He walked to her.

"You're right. I was the one who asked for it because I saw no other way."

Nate took the cup from her hand and placed it on the counter. "How about we table the divorce for now? You know, work on things. I know we're worth saving."

She moved closer to him. "I think that might be a good idea."

He hugged her tight. "Noelle's going to have a sibling. She'll be so happy. She's tired of doing all the work around here." He squeezed Nikki hard and kissed her with the love she missed.

She was dizzy from the intensity of his passion and moved him away slightly. "That still leaves the matter of finances."

If she could take those words back, she would have. She'd never learned how to not kill the moment.

"How about we celebrate the fact that we're having a baby and might not be getting divorced? Deal?"

She shook her head and liked the idea.

"Uh-oh. Sorry to interrupt." Tara crashed their reconciliation.

Nate backed away. "No problem. We were catching up." His hand slid down her arm and into her hand.

"I wanted to tell you what a beautiful song that was. I hope you don't mind that I didn't sing the rest of it. It's beautiful, but maybe a little inappropriate for this wedding. Let them learn about the hardship of marriage on their own." Tara laughed.

"The song." Nikki had been so caught up in her pregnancy that she completely forgot about the song. "How did you know about it?"

Tara motioned to Nate.

"I found your notebook on the bed. It was open, so it's not like I was snooping. I brought it to Tara and asked what she thought of it."

"It's terrific. So much that I want to know if you're open to a collaboration. My music, your lyrics."

Nikki froze. Now she was sure her stomach was churning because an award-winning musician was asking her if she could use *her* lyrics. "You mean, like an actual professional collaboration?"

"Absolutely. I think you've got something. I'd like to hear the rest of the song you were humming the other day."

She felt faint. She and Tara Graham writing together.

"Are you kidding me?" She wanted to jump out of her skin. "Um, I think that would work great if you don't mind working with a novice." Her head was spinning. All those months spent unsure of her future and the one person she'd thought she'd lost was the one who brought it all together for her. Tara would never have read her song if it wasn't for Nate. She held his hand with enough love to make up for the time they'd lost. But it wasn't just the song. She really did love him, but couldn't figure out how to make it right. When her voice failed her, the written words didn't.

Tara poured a glass of wine from the sideboard. "Want some?"

"No." Nikki shook her head.

"Definitely." Nate reached for a glass.

"I'm glad you brought up novices. Not that I think you're one, but I've been wanting to create a foundation for unknown musicians and songwriters. I'd like to set up a retreat where they can create without the distraction of unwanted stimulation that kills their creative process." Tara took a sip of wine. "I think you know what I mean." She stared at Nikki.

"I do."

"I think this place would be perfect. Would you be open to renting it out for a set period of time for a project like that?"

Nikki pulled Nate in close to her and rubbed her belly. His look gave her the answer she needed. "I think it would be the perfect solution for our family."

It Was You
by Lita Harris

It was you who made me see.
The beginning of a new me.
I didn't know back then that it would never end.
I only wanted to love you and have you next to me.

You showed me what I never knew.
And that was to spend my life with you.
Here we are years later with a deeper desire,
But can't find our way back through the fire.

As many doors opened, more closed behind us.
Dreams shattered, hope faded, it was all a bust.
I sit here searching for an answer.
No more hurt, a gentle hint of closure.

We've been through so much.
All I want is to feel your touch.
To find our way back to the past.
Whatever the future may cast.

About…

Lita Harris spends her time between New Jersey and the Endless Mountains region of Pennsylvania, where she writes most of her books. She also lived in Alaska for a short time just for fun. An avid crafter, unused supplies clutter her basement and attempts at making pottery, jewelry, and stained glass are proudly displayed in her house, usually behind a picture or holding a door open. She also makes candles and homemade soap. With enough books to stock a small library she may need to construct a building to store her literary obsessions.

She writes in multiple genres, including women's fiction, contemporary romance, paranormal, and cozy mysteries.

♥♥♥

For more information about Lita, please visit her website at www.LitaHarris.com or at twitter.com/litaharris and facebook.com/litaharrisauthor.

For more stories by Lita Harris, try *Love at Christmas,* Available now from Sweet Cravings Publishing.

♥♥♥

Love at Christmas

Kristen Anderson is resigned to live a child-free life in New Jersey. That is, until she's given custody of her seven-year-old nephew after the death of his mother. Christmas brings them to their grandmother's house in Pennsylvania where the family focuses on healing and reopening the family inn in time for the holidays. Enter Luke Baldwin, a man with a past that leaves him uncertain whether he'll ever find love—until he meets Kristen.

Kristen's and Luke's desire to be together is complicated by Kristen's yearning to return to New Jersey, her grandmother's determination to keep Kristen in Brookside Falls, and a family secret that is revealed on Christmas Eve. Will the deceit that threatens to break them apart change their lives forever? What will Christmas bring them?

♥♥♥

To Have
and to Hold

Emma Kaye

♥♥♥

Viv and Gabe Ganivet have returned to The Loon Lake Inn for their fifteenth wedding anniversary in an effort to save their crumbling marriage. It's been two years since the death of their son and they're struggling to recover some semblance of a normal life.

When a meddling ghost sends them back in time to their wedding weekend, will they find a way to regain some of what they've lost? Or did their ghostly "friend" have something else in mind?

♥♥♥

Dedicated to ~

My husband—I couldn't have found a better man "to have and to hold" and am eternally grateful I get to spend my life with you.

My family—I love you with all my heart. I'm so lucky to be a part of your lives.

Ruth, Lita, Nicole, Julie, Desi, and Mallory—Our Tuesday night hangouts are a highlight of my week. Y'all are awesome.

To Have and to Hold
by Emma Kaye

"We can't go on this way."

Viv Ganivet rolled onto her side and pulled the comforter over her shoulder. Her husband's tone of voice tore at her heartstrings. He was right. She knew it. But she couldn't force herself to do anything about it.

He hovered over her. Would he go away, or was he going to push her on this?

Today of all days.

Tears burned behind her lids.

"I'm tired. Can we do this tomorrow?" she asked, hating the whiny tone in her voice.

Gabe snorted. "That's what you said yesterday." He tugged at the comforter. "Take a shower. We'll grab some—" he looked at his watch, "—dinner and talk."

Her fist tightened around the corner of the blanket, but he yanked it from her grasp.

So…now it is. Her stomach tightened into a knot. She

didn't want to hear what he was going to say. She'd been expecting it for a while. Why did he have to pick today?

She sat and brushed her hair out of her face. His frown brought fresh tears to her eyes. She averted her gaze so he wouldn't see. She didn't want his comfort right now.

How he must hate her. She was nothing like her old self. She never used to cry at the drop of a hat, or sleep all day to avoid facing the world.

He was still the amazing man she'd married. More so. While he'd been a tower of strength these past two years, she'd completely fallen apart. And couldn't seem to pull herself back together no matter how much she wanted to.

That he'd stayed with her this long continued to amaze her.

He moved out of her way, so she tottered to the bathroom and straight into the hot shower he'd started for her. She turned up the heat until it fairly scalded her skin, the jets of water pounding upon her head. The Loon Lake Inn had made some upgrades in the fifteen years since she and Gabe had gotten married there. The water pressure had been horrible back then.

She made quick work of cleaning herself, but stayed until the water had cooled uncomfortably, with the vain hope that her husband would have given up and left.

No such luck.

When she blindly reached from behind the curtain to feel her way to a dry towel, one was thrust into her hand.

Apparently Gabe was determined to have that talk. She knew all his moods. None of her tricks were going to work—because he knew her just as well.

She finished drying and wrapped the towel around her body like a shield before stepping out to face him. But he wasn't there.

Rustling noises came from the bedroom. A peek through the steam revealed him pulling clothes out of her suitcase and laying them out on the rumpled hotel comforter.

Sweat beaded on her upper lip. The thick air of the bathroom made breathing a struggle. Her heartbeat raced. What would she do if he'd finally had enough?

He was just as handsome as he'd been all those years ago. More, actually. His dark hair was sprinkled with gray, his belly was a little softer, and lines fanned out from the corners of his eyes—but it all added a mature, confident quality that drew people to him.

Herself included. She just didn't know how to reach out. Whenever she tried, she ended up snapping at him. She'd regret it immediately, but too late to erase the damage. He'd say everything was all right, but she could always see the hurt in his eyes.

Nothing was all right anymore.

They'd lost so much. Was she about to lose Gabe, too?

Before he could turn and catch her staring, she swung around to the mirror and fumbled through the array of toiletries spread out on the counter. He'd mentioned dinner—he probably wanted to have this conversation in public so she wouldn't break down or leave.

Time to put on her face. She made quick work of her hair and makeup—she almost never bothered anymore. She'd cut her hair short, so drying took only a minute or two. A dusting of blush, a quick swipe of eyeliner and lip gloss. All done. With the towel tucked securely around her breasts, she went to get dressed.

He clicked off the TV and rose from his chair. His navy blue slacks were neatly pressed, as was his white button-down shirt. He'd kept busy while she showered.

The ironing board stood in the corner and one of her blouses hung off the edge, no wrinkles to be seen. She hadn't been wrinkle free in two years.

She couldn't make herself care.

Her underwear and khaki pants slipped on easily beneath the towel, but she turned her back to him to put on her bra. She hooked the strap in place and dropped the towel on the edge of the bed. She didn't face him again until her blouse was buttoned almost to the top.

The hungry look in his gaze kicked her guilt up a notch to twist like a knife in her stomach.

She hadn't always been so shy. The added pounds and stretch marks from pregnancy hadn't done it. Not in front of him, at least. He'd once kissed the white lines on her belly and told her how they reminded him that she was the mother of his child and how much he loved them both.

Now that Connor was gone…they were just ugly marks on her body that reminded her she no longer had the child who made them. She wasn't a mother anymore. She didn't deserve that badge of accomplishment.

"Come on, let's go. I made a reservation for seven. It's five of."

Gabe's voice jolted her out of her thoughts. He stood there holding open the door, staring at her, one eyebrow raised. Had he asked her to leave more than once?

He ushered her out of the room and straight to the glass elevator. She looked out on the gazebo that was draped with twinkling lights and hundreds of flowers. A happy bride and groom posed for pictures as the inn's staff put the finishing touches on the outdoor reception area. The setting sun reflected off the lake's glassy surface in the distance.

The silence in the elevator was suffocating.

Memories of her own wedding flashed through her mind, along with a dream she'd had the night before.

"I dreamed of your great-aunt last night." She winced. She might as well have shouted.

"Agnes? She's been dead for—what—six years? Why'd you dream of her?"

"No idea." She wrinkled her brow in thought. "It was really weird. She apologized and said she'd found a way to make it right."

"Make what right?"

She shrugged. "She didn't say. She said something about a mistake and the gazebo, but I can't quite remember…"

His warmth soaked into her back, contrasting with the slight chill of the glass against her hand. She hadn't realized she'd pressed herself against the elevator wall while she took in the beauty of the view.

"We were so happy back then," he said.

She nodded.

"You were gorgeous in your dress. I swear my heart stopped when I got my first glimpse of you walking down the aisle."

She pictured him standing at the steps of the gazebo, a star-struck look on his face. He used to have a way of looking at her that made her feel like she was the only person in the entire world. "I remember." It had been a while since she'd seen that look. Lately it seemed they avoided each other's eyes more often than not.

"Good. I know you didn't want to come, especially this weekend."

Tension gripped her body tight in its grasp. She rubbed a hand over her stomach, remembering what it had felt like being pregnant. She'd been overjoyed when Connor was born on their anniversary, even though a part of her had missed that feeling of him growing within her.

Her body had kept him safe then.

But she'd ultimately failed in that respect, hadn't she?

She hadn't been able to protect him in the end.

"But I think Dr. Barstow was right to suggest we come back here. We need to remember the good things, too. Not just the bad."

"How?" She turned to face him, startled to find herself pressed tight to his chest. She stepped to the side. "How do you do that? Because I can't." She wrapped her arms around herself, rocking back and forth on the balls of her feet. She missed Gabe's warmth. Why couldn't she bring herself to sink into his arms like she wanted?

"We can make new memories."

We?

He took a deep breath and her stomach sank. He was about to bring up something she might not like. "We're still relatively young. We can have another baby."

A buzzing in her head drowned out the rest of his words. His mouth continued to move, but she couldn't hear what he said. The next noise that registered was the smack of her hand against his cheek.

♥♥♥

Two hours later, Viv stared up at the gazebo. A cool breeze brushed across her heated face. She'd run until she had a stitch in her side and found herself further from the inn than she'd ever been. The walk back had exhausted her. Thank goodness the trails were well marked.

The wedding reception was in full swing. The chairs from the ceremony had been removed, and everyone partied under the white canvas tent set up close to the pool area. The music was loud and the drinks flowed at the open bar. Happy people danced and laughed. No one paid any attention to this lovely spot where one of the most important moments of Viv's life had occurred.

A figure came out from the shadows. She wasn't scared. The spicy scent of his aftershave—and her body's instinctive pull toward him—told her it was Gabe waiting in the dark. The tension that had drained from her body, leaving her weak and tired but sad rather than angry, surged through her spine once more. She threw her shoulders back and glared.

"Where've you been?" he asked in a tired voice. "I was worried."

And just like that she was drained once more. She wanted to reach out to him, take him in her arms and hold him until his voice resonated with the strength and happiness he'd once known. Back when they'd exchanged their vows in the very spot where he now stood.

"I wandered around. Hiked along the nature trail." She put one foot on the first step, turning her ankle so the light illuminated the dirt-encrusted, inch-high heel on her sandals. "Not such a great plan."

"You can't avoid me forever."

No, but she'd been trying. "You surprised me earlier. I thought you wanted a divorce. Not a—a baby." She winced. The idea brought a crazy jumble of emotions to the surface. She fought the urge to slap him again and shoved aside all those feelings. Locked them away, like she'd been doing for two years.

"I can't do this anymore," he whispered.

He might as well have shouted. The words slammed into her like bullets.

"I don't know what to do. Something needs change. We need to move forward. We at least need to start talking." He held out his hand. "I don't want a divorce, but…"

Her hand trembled when she placed it in his. Could she give him what he needed? Part of her screamed to go to him, do whatever it took to keep him. But another part had already run away, hidden deep in the shadows of her heart. He'd want all of her. Gabe would never be satisfied with less.

He deserved so much more.

She couldn't meet his eyes. Her gaze remained riveted on her feet as he helped her up the steps.

A wave of dizziness washed over her. She tried to focus on their feet. They stood toe-to-toe, his rounded loafers clean and scuff free, her bare toes peeking out of strappy sandals. Her unpolished nails blurred.

Her eyelids drooped. So heavy. She fought to keep them open. Her knees buckled. A white haze obscured her vision.

"Viv." Gabe's panicked cry reached her ears less than a second before they both crumpled to the ground.

♥♥♥

"Drunk, I take it?"

Viv winced as a vaguely familiar, querulous man's voice pierced her aching head. *Who was he talking about?* Had some of the inn's guests gotten rowdy? The reception noises had receded and all she could hear was a man and woman arguing.

The woman's voice was less grating on her nerves. She spoke softly, so Viv couldn't really hear what was said, only a soft murmur in a light tone.

The cold planks of the gazebo floor pressed against Viv's spine. A faint hint of copper and a swelling in her mouth told her she'd bitten the inside of her cheek.

"Go on, Agnes. See if you can get them up. You don't want some drunk idiots ruining your great-nephew's wedding."

Someone shook her shoulder gently. She forced her eyes open and saw an old woman peering down at her. The fog shrouding Viv's mind prevented her from coming up with a name, but she could swear she recognized the lady.

"What happened?" She squinted into the night. Haphazardly placed lanterns lit colorful gardens. One hung nearby, its light shining directly in her eyes. "Where's my husband?"

"Over there. Fall-down drunk, just like you. You'd think you two would be old enough to handle your drink," the cranky male voice said.

Viv swiveled around and found Gabe a few feet away, struggling to sit. He held a hand to his head and looked as confused as she felt. *Was he hurt?* A vise gripped her chest. The old woman's hand on her arm prevented her from going to him.

The woman peered over her shoulder at the man. "I don't smell alcohol on them." She returned her attention to Viv. "You two have some kind of accident? Do you need a doctor?"

"They need an AA meeting, not a doctor, Agnes." He dug his hands into his pockets. A scowl deepened the already thick wrinkles lining his mouth. Rather than making him look as fierce as his tone of voice, he appeared confused. Viv wanted to reassure him everything was all right.

"Now I need a drink." Agnes rolled her eyes, then smiled at Viv. "Don't mind Albert. Can't take a sip of alcohol without him calling AA. Doesn't seem to stop him from imbibing, mind you. The old pain in the ass." The fond smile she cast her husband belied the nastiness of her words. She squinted over Viv's shoulder. "You two look so familiar. Do I know you?"

Albert? Agnes? Now that's strange. Viv peered more closely at the couple. They even looked like Gabe's relatives.

Gabe was suddenly behind her, his hands under her armpits hauling her to her feet. "You okay?"

No. She nodded. "Fine. What's going on? Did you faint, too?"

Albert and Agnes watched, their aged faces curious.

Gabe draped an arm over her shoulder and squeezed. But instead of answering her questions, he spoke to the old couple. "We're fine. Thanks for the help. We should go get cleaned up." He steered her toward the inn.

She barely managed a weak wave before he dragged her away. "What was that all about? Why did you run away like that? I wanted to find out who they are. Did you notice how much they looked like Agnes and Albert? Same names and everything. It's weird."

They'd reached the pool area. Floating candles cast a romantic glow on the still waters. The rush of the waterfall at the far end blocked out noises from guests milling about the bar area inside. Through the wall of glass, she could see some sort of party going on.

Gabe stepped a few feet away from her and glanced at his watch. He mumbled to himself, then swung back toward her, a serious expression on his face. He pulled two Adirondack chairs to face each other and gestured for her to have a seat.

"We need to talk," he said in a strained voice.

Now? He wanted to have their talk now? "Don't you think we should call a doctor? We both just fainted for no reason. Something's wrong." After everything they'd been through, now they might have some kind of health issue?

No. She couldn't take it. She couldn't.

"Yeah, I know. But I think I know what happened."

"What? Were we exposed to something? Are we sick?" Nausea turned her stomach. Was it real, or was she reacting to the idea? Felt real enough.

"No, nothing like that." He squeezed her shoulder. He pulled a stick of gum from his pocket and stuck it in his mouth, chewing for a moment before sighing and spitting it into the wrapper.

A sure sign he was stressed. He was probably itching for a cigarette right about now. The gum was his backup plan. She'd made him quit years ago when he'd asked her to marry him. Smoking was a deal breaker for her.

She waited him out. If they were going to do this, she wasn't going to make it any harder on herself by putting her foot in her mouth before he had a chance to say boo. He'd already brought up the *D* word—she wasn't going to push it.

Maybe she was jumping to conclusions? They might not be sick, but *something* weird was going on. He couldn't ignore that fact.

Her patience wasn't going to last forever, though. Her fingers twitched where she clutched them tight in her lap. Why didn't he say anything? Instead, he stared at his knees, chewing yet another piece of gum.

A door opened and noise filtered out to them. She craned her neck to get a glimpse, but he shifted and blocked her view.

"Do you remember me telling you about my aunt Agnes's rather *unusual* religious beliefs?"

"Sure. Raised Wiccan, but converted to Catholicism to marry Albert. She believed in everything and nothing, all at once." *Crazy old bat.* Agnes was the only one in Gabe's family who never completely warmed up to her. Viv had given up trying to win her favor after a few choice remarks the weekend they got married. They'd eventually come to a grudging mutual respect, but no real affection.

"That about sums it up. Only she never gave up her witchy ways. I always thought it was a bunch of crap, but now I'm not so sure."

"Why now? Because I had that stupid dream?"

"Yes. And because that *was* Agnes and Albert we saw just a few moments ago."

She snorted. "Right. They suddenly came back to life to wish us a happy anniversary." She was in no mood for bad jokes. "What's wrong with you?" Why was he acting like this? Had he finally cracked under the pressure?

"I'm serious."

She didn't doubt it. Frown lines drew down the corners of his mouth, his brows were furrowed, and his gaze was intense as he stared somewhere in the vicinity of her knees. He always avoided eye contact until the moment he blurted out whatever was bothering him. He was gathering his thoughts. Once he looked into her eyes, he wouldn't turn away until he'd finished.

He finally met her gaze and her breath caught.

He *was* serious, but there was an uncertainty in his gaze she hated seeing. He didn't think she'd believe him.

But how could she? He was trying to make her believe his aunt and uncle had miraculously returned from the dead.

"Agnes and Albert died six years ago, within a few months of each other. That couldn't possibly be them." Was this some kind of loyalty test? Did he expect her to believe him no matter what insane story he came up with?

Just a few years ago, she would have. His word would have been enough for her—no matter how far-fetched. The thought made her chest ache.

"And yet it was." His voice was frustratingly calm.

He rarely lost his temper. Nothing rattled him anymore. "Have you noticed anything else around here? Like this pool? Or the gazebo?"

What is he getting at? She scanned the area around them with a frown. *Huh.* "It must be the light. The stonework looks different." Nikki's daughter, Noelle— twenty-seven now and engaged to be married—had taken them around to show off all the changes they'd made the past few years, the pool area being one of them. Yet everything looked exactly as she remembered it from their wedding.

Exactly. Down to the floating candles and new rosebushes. Her eyes widened. Thoughts whirled chaotically through her head. Nothing stayed exactly the same for fifteen years.

She could have sworn the bushes were three times this size. The gazebo had been different, too. Freshly planted rosebushes, bare wires where a light used to be, and a ladder tucked along the far rail indicated some kind of repair was going on.

But Noelle had mentioned the gazebo had received a fresh coat of paint last week to be ready for a wedding.

What she was thinking wasn't possible. She misunderstood what Gabe was trying to tell her. She did that more often than not lately.

"Look closely." Gabe slipped to the side a few inches and gestured toward the bar. A few people had come out into the cool night air and lingered around the edges of the pool opposite where they sat.

She couldn't get a good look at any of them, yet they seemed familiar somehow. Someone shifted to the side and she gasped. She raised a trembling hand to point at the woman who had come into view. "That's the crazy lady who crashed our wedding weekend. I remember that godawful slutty dress—I spilled a vodka cranberry on her that first night we all spent at the inn. I felt so guilty for ruining it. But then she was such a bitch about it. I was *pissed*. Remember?"

She'd been doing shots with the girls and had been none too steady on her feet.

He nodded. "Yeah. She threw a fit, then lied her way into my friend's room later." He laughed. "Lots of drama that—uh, this—weekend. But…Viv." He took her hand and squeezed. "I don't think Agnes was a dream. You saw her ghost. And she sent us back in time to the weekend we got married."

The crowd parted and she had a straight line of sight to the bar. Holy crap. Her breath came in short gasps. She was going to hyperventilate.

Through the crowds of people, she could see— herself.

"Why?" A hundred questions ran through her mind. *Why* was the only one short enough to make it out of her mouth.

The answer hit her before he had a chance to come up with a reply. "She said she was going to fix things." Agnes had tried to talk Gabe out of marrying her. She'd told him Viv was "flighty" and would never be a proper wife to him. "She thinks we made a mistake getting married."

No. No. No. It can't be…

The chair scraped the backs of her legs when she jumped to her feet. The scratch registered as a mild sting. A distant part of her brain told her she should take a look at it. She didn't. She had to get out of here.

A sharp pain hit her chest. She couldn't breathe. "Agnes sent us back so we can stop the wedding."

No. Her mind kept repeating the word over and over. She didn't want that. Did Gabe?

♥♥♥

Viv ignored Gabe yelling after her. She ran away from the crowds of people at the bar. Not just any people. All her friends and relatives from fifteen years ago.

She'd lost touch with many of them since Connor's death. Not that they hadn't tried to talk to her, but Viv had cut herself off. She hadn't wanted to know how much Morgan and Margot's kids enjoyed spending summers on Star Island with their cousins, or hear about Nikki and Nate's teenage son's latest wrestling win. Getting the happy family photo Christmas cards every year was torture enough.

The last one she'd mailed was two and a half years ago. Connor had been only six years old.

She took the glass elevator up to her room on the second floor. She would open the door, see their luggage spread about the room, and prove Gabe was wrong about the whole time-travel nonsense.

She hadn't seen her younger self at the bar. Her eyes had played tricks on her.

It took her three tries to get the old-fashioned key into the lock, her hands shook so violently. She'd thought it quaint that they still had actual keys instead of cards. Noelle had explained how they'd gone to great lengths to make the keys look old, when they'd actually modernized the locks to provide the best security to keep their guests safe.

The handle refused to budge. She tried again.

And again.

Same result.

This can't be happening. It's impossible.

She didn't believe in this nonsense.

Besides, Agnes had come around a few years after

the wedding. She saw that Viv and Gabe had the same passion for each other as on the day they married. They hadn't exactly been best friends, but Viv had received a reluctant stamp of approval in the form of Agnes's recipe for Gabe's favorite apple pie.

If time travel was possible, Agnes wouldn't try to break up Viv and Gabe. She wouldn't.

Would she?

Maybe she thought to spare them the anguish of losing their son.

Viv choked back a sob and spun away from the locked door.

No. She wouldn't allow it. No matter how awful life was without Connor, Viv couldn't do that to her son. Gabe wouldn't want that, either.

She took the stairs to the lobby, afraid she'd run into someone she knew. What would she say? What would they think?

She didn't want to find out.

A glance at her watch told her it was 1:00 a.m. The party would be breaking up about now, if she remembered correctly. Her friends would be stumbling back to their rooms.

Gabe leaned on the reception desk next to a gorgeous display of colorful wildflowers, smiling as Nikki handed him a key. If this truly were their wedding weekend, he had just worked wonders. They'd pretty much booked the entire inn with all their guests. How had he managed to get a room?

Judging by the adoring look on Nikki's face, he'd charmed it out of her. Viv wanted to rip the woman's hair out. Which was ridiculous since Nikki was a friend *and* happily married.

He turned and caught sight of her. He rushed over to usher her down the hall and into the billiard room. At this time of night, it was blessedly empty, but the lingering scent of cigars and spilled beer reminded her that Gabe and his boys had spent—would spend?—quite a few hours playing pool this weekend.

"How'd you get a room? Aren't they booked solid?"

"I told Nikki we were cousins of the groom." He gestured to his face. "She didn't have any trouble believing I was related. And I lucked out because Agnes happened by and swore I was cousin Jimmy."

"Did Agnes curse you or hug you? With all the drama between Jimmy's mom and your dad, I've never met him." She'd heard the story over the years, of course. She knew all Gabe's stories. His dad and aunt hadn't gotten along since their parents died and his aunt made off with just about everything of value in the house while Gabe's dad had been dealing with the funeral arrangements. It had been a bitter parting of ways, to say the least.

"Me, either. But Agnes decided I must have come to make the peace. She promised to save us seats at the rehearsal tomorrow night."

"Great." Viv rolled her eyes. "We'll just stroll in—"

"Shh." He put a finger over her lips. "Someone's coming," he whispered.

She strained to hear what he was talking about. A giggle, followed by a throaty laugh sounded right outside the door.

Her eyes went wide. "That's us," she hissed at him.

His head swiveled back and forth. His eyes scanned the room. "We have to hide." He grabbed her arm and dragged her to a door she hadn't noticed in the corner.

He yanked it open and pushed her inside. The closet barely had enough room for the two of them. Shelves lined each side, piled high with games on one half and plastic storage bins on the other.

They squeezed into the narrow area in the center. They hadn't been this close in ages. Every inch of their bodies was forced together to fit into the tight space. Every breath she took pushed her breasts tighter to his chest and sent a tingle straight through her. The warmth of his breath added a flame to her already burning cheeks.

He pulled the door shut and plunged them into absolute darkness. The faint hint of light lining the bottom and top of the door did nothing to aid her sight.

His hand rested against her thigh where the doorknob jutted into her rear. She tried not to notice how she could feel every line of his hard body.

Or that a certain part of him was growing noticeably harder.

She concentrated on the sounds coming from the other room. Their younger selves made a drunken effort to whisper, which meant they could be heard clear as day.

"Stop that. I'm still angry with you." Young Viv tried to sound stern, but the laughter in her voice ruined the effect.

Viv had forgotten her tendency to giggle when she got drunk.

"Aw, come on, baby. I made a joke. What's the big deal?"

She rolled her eyes at the pleading note in young Gabe's voice. He used to think he was being charming, but it always seemed more like begging to her. All in all, she'd been rather fond of it because it usually led to great makeup sex.

"Some joke. You asked for tips on how to get laid more often."

"I was kidding. Nobody took me seriously. Besides, there's no way. Two or three times every day? She was drunk and exaggerating."

Her younger self giggled. "I knew she was drunk. I

just didn't realize she was *that* drunk."

"Oh, yeah. He's got his hands full trying to work things out with her tonight."

There was a slight thump, followed by more giggling and rustling noises.

"Oh, shit," Gabe said under his breath.

"What?"

"Don't you remember? After the party let out?"

Viv tried to remember. It was a long time ago, and she hadn't exactly remained sober that weekend. "We had a fight…" She hadn't remembered until now what the fight had been about, only that they'd had a major blowout days before the wedding.

It all seemed so trivial now. But back then, they'd fought so rarely, even a minor disagreement had seemed like a big deal. They hadn't been able to stay mad at each other for long.

They rarely fought now, either, but only because Gabe walked on eggshells around her.

He wrapped her in his arms, distracting her from her thoughts. How could she remember the past, when he was pressed so tightly against her now? He shifted and his erection rubbed against her stomach. She stifled a groan.

It had been a really long time.

"I can't remember what we fought about, but I remember making up," he whispered.

The heat of his breath sent goose bumps chasing down her arm. She tilted her head and his hand cupped the back of her neck. He pressed light kisses against the sensitive spot behind her ear.

A loud groan from their younger selves startled her. She'd almost forgotten why they were stuck in this tiny closet.

"Someone could walk in on us."

Her younger self's statement echoed her thoughts.

Did she want to be caught hiding in a closet? How exactly would they explain that?

"Who cares?" younger Gabe asked.

She'd forgotten how he'd gotten off on the threat of discovery. She had, too, if she were honest. She'd just enjoyed having Gabe work for it a little. He'd call her a tease, and she'd play it up.

She missed those days. Nothing else had mattered but each other.

Nausea rose up her throat and the bitter taste of bile hit the back of her tongue. She was going to be sick. What kind of a mother was she? How could she have forgotten, for a second, why those times had become a thing of the past?

She struggled to breathe. She had to get out of here. She couldn't...

Gabe stopped kissing her. His touch became comforting, rather than sexual. "Are you okay? What's wrong?"

A huge lump in her throat prevented her reply. She shook her head and forced her hands between them to push against his chest.

Room. She needed room.

"*Shh. Shh.*" He inched away, giving her a tiny bit of breathing room. "Just another minute. Remember? We were caught, um, red-handed."

Laughter was clear in his voice. She clapped a hand over her mouth. She didn't know if she was going to laugh or cry as the memory returned. Gabe stroked her arm and a bit of the hysteria retreated until she knew she wouldn't betray their presence with sound.

She couldn't believe she'd forgotten. The inn's owner, Nate, had caught them in the act. Gabe with his pants unbuckled and drooping down his hips. Her propped on the edge of the pool table, legs wrapped around his waist. She'd been mortified, but thankful he hadn't come in a second or two later and gotten a real show.

The creak of a door opening was followed swiftly by her younger self's shriek. Viv was grateful she couldn't see Gabe's face in the dark. Fine tremors of suppressed mirth passed through his body. He'd found the whole thing hilarious back then, too. She could hear young Gabe's laughter as her younger self fumbled with her clothing and Nate mumbled an agonized apology before slamming the door shut.

Their younger selves quickly gathered themselves together and stumbled away to their room. They'd gotten over their embarrassment fairly quickly and spent an amazingly athletic evening in their room. Viv could remember a fleeting desire to abstain for a month before their wedding night, but had passed off the thought as temporary insanity. They'd been so hot for each other back then, they'd thoroughly enjoyed their wedding night, despite having had a sex marathon only two nights before.

She shook off the memory as they waited to be sure Nate didn't return so they could come out of hiding. Gabe inched the door open slowly and peered into the room. She lurched out of the closet, sucking in huge lungfuls of air. She bent at the waist, hands on her knees.

Gabe rubbed her back. Brushed her hair out of her eyes. "Let's get some sleep. We can figure everything out in the morning." Taking care of her. Like always.

God, she was a freakin' mess.

♥♥♥

Viv woke with a throbbing headache. Gabe snored softly beside her. His arm slung over her hip, his legs tucked behind hers. His warmth pulled her in, but the urgent needs of her waking body prodded her out of bed.

She got ready in record time. She didn't exactly have a choice in clothing, so she slipped back into her blouse and pants from yesterday. Gabe had hung them up for her, so they didn't look all that awful. In usual caring form, he'd also managed to find some ibuprofen and had the bottle on the counter next to the water glasses. Her head always bothered her after one of her panic attacks.

He was too good to be true. She was such a bitch and he continued to take care of her. Sometimes she wanted to slap him. How did he do it? He went to work, socialized with his colleagues, stayed in touch with friends, and looked after her. She went through the motions of life—work, eat, sleep—but she wasn't living. How could he continue on as if their world hadn't ended?

A knock on the door startled her out of her thoughts. Her body tensed. Who could be looking for them here? Now?

She sneaked over to the peephole to take a peek outside.

Agnes stood on the other side of the door, a porter behind her carrying several garment bags. *What the...?*

Viv grabbed the baseball cap Gabe had bought at the gift shop yesterday and yanked it down over her eyes. If they'd been outside, she'd have put on the sunglasses, too, but she figured that would be overkill since they were inside. She'd keep her head tilted down so Agnes couldn't get a good look at her face.

The safety lock on the door took a moment to undo,

but she finally managed to get the door open to stare in shock at her husband's great-aunt.

"Oh, good. You're awake." Agnes didn't try to hide her curious glance into their room. "Well, mostly." She smiled. "Jimmy mentioned that the airline lost your luggage so I borrowed a few things so you could get yourself all fancied up for the rehearsal tonight and the wedding tomorrow." She waved the porter forward and held up a hand when Viv started to speak. "Hush, now. No need to thank me. We're family, after all. And Lord knows how members of this family love to overpack. It wasn't any trouble. I'll expect to see you at the rehearsal. I arranged everything with the inn. You'll be at my table."

The porter placed the garment bags on a wing chair and left. Agnes gave a jaunty little wave and followed after him, shutting the door behind her.

Viv stared at the fire escape route posted below the peephole. *What just happened?* She'd had an entire conversation and hadn't said one word. Agnes had blown in and out, leaving Viv stumbling for balance in her wake, trying to catch her breath.

"She's a force of nature sometimes." Gabe spoke from the bed.

Viv turned to face her husband. He sat propped against the headboard. The sheet draped across his lap, his chest bare. He looked good. His salt-and-pepper hair stood out all over his head. He could use a haircut, but she liked the unkempt look.

He'd gained a lot of weight immediately after losing Connor. Drinking and eating had taken the place of sports and camping. But for the past year, he'd been hitting the gym pretty hard. She could see the results.

He was moving on with his life, while she wasn't.

She forced her eyes to stay on his face. She was not going to ogle her husband. "Yeah. She probably thinks

I'm mute. I couldn't get a word in. On a positive side, she likes me more as Jimmy's wife than she ever did as yours."

"That's not true. She loved you." He didn't sound entirely convinced.

She snorted. "Bull. She decided to tolerate me when we didn't divorce right away." They'd made peace with each other, but there'd always been a bit of residual tension.

Gabe got out of bed and strolled over. He wore nothing but boxers slung low on his hips. She fought to keep her breathing steady when he stopped right next to her. She kept her back rigid and grabbed one of the garment bags, hanging it up in the closet then struggling with the zipper.

He sighed. With a quick jerk, he got the zipper started, then turned and took care of the second bag.

"I'm not sure I want to see what she expects us to wear." Agnes favored kitten prints and flannel leggings. Hopefully she'd borrowed from one of their more stylish family members.

"Nice," he said, pulling out a charcoal-gray suit, lavender button-down shirt, and striped tie. He checked the tag. "Might be a little snug, but it will do."

She held her breath as she checked out her options. Not bad. She fingered the silky material of a black wraparound with a large red flower print. The flower was placed perfectly to disguise the flab around her middle. Size? Close enough. A little big, but that was probably a good thing with that clingy fabric. At least she wouldn't be stuffing her extra inches into a tight little sheath dress. This would fit well enough so she wouldn't make a spectacle of herself. She released her breath in a rush.

Speaking of spectacles, she better find herself a floppy hat to hide her face or someone was bound to notice her resemblance to her younger self. That would certainly up the drama level of her wedding.

Her wedding—one of the happiest moments of her life. She couldn't ruin it. She couldn't. For Connor, of course. And Gabe. Despite everything, she couldn't imagine her life without him. Didn't want to.

"What are we going to do? We can't stay here forever. Do you think Agnes will send us back if we…" She closed her eyes and rushed on, "…if we don't stop the wedding?"

He put a hand on her shoulder and forced her to face him. "You're wrong. I know it. Maybe she just wants to remind us why we got married in the first place. That we've made a mistake letting ourselves grow apart these last years."

She grimaced and clenched her fists at her side. "You're saying she thinks it's my fault." *Was she right?*

"That's not what I said." He threw his hands up. "Damn it, Viv. I can't say anything right. You jump down my throat."

She wrapped her arms around her midsection. "I'm sorry," she mumbled. "I'm confused and freaked out. I don't know what to think about any of this."

He gave her a quick hug. Before she could return it, he let her go. Did he think she'd push him away? Funny. Yesterday she probably would have. Today, she wished he'd held on longer.

"I know. I'm kinda freaked myself," he said. "Let me get dressed. We'll go down and check out the gazebo. Maybe there's a way to get back that we overlooked."

"And if we don't find anything?"

His mouth was set in grim lines. "I'll think of something."

♥♥♥

They spent the better part of the day scouring the grounds and trying to check out the gazebo without being noticed by their families. Thankfully, part of the weekend itinerary had been a nature hike led by their old friend Todd—so life became a bit easier once most of the guests left.

Not that the freedom to roam got them anywhere. Viv ended up hot, tired, and no closer to figuring out how to get home. She flopped onto the top step of the gazebo. A second later, Gabe sat beside her.

"What are we going to do?" She caught her head in her hands, bracing her elbows on her knees.

"I think we should talk to Agnes." He leaned in, his shoulder pressed against hers, the scent of his gum minty fresh.

She brought her head up slowly. "Why? She doesn't know who we are. Or do you have some way of contacting her ghost?" She regretted her snotty tone the second it came out. He was doing his best in a crazy situation. He didn't deserve her scorn.

He backed away, then stood before her, though he kept his gaze toward the inn. "She may not know what's going on, but she could know how it's possible."

"Fine. Let's go." Getting to her feet took more effort than it should have. All she wanted to do was curl up and forget everything. Particularly the hurt look in his eyes right now.

Why did she have to be such a bitch to him? Her throat clogged with all the loving things she should say to him, but never seemed to make it past her lips. There was so much to say. Where to start?

She put a hand on his shoulder. Tears clouded her

vision when he flinched. *Damn*. "I'm sorry, Gabe. I don't know why I act this way. You deserve so much better."

His lips curled in a faint smile and the pain in his eyes lessened. "Hey, none of that." He put his arm around her shoulder and pulled her to his side. "For better or for worse, right?"

"I'm the worse; you're the better."

"We're having a tough time," he whispered. "We're gonna get through it. I know we will."

She wished she could believe him.

They made their way in silence back to the inn. They'd watched Todd take his nature group out on the hike, so they knew Agnes wasn't among them.

She'd almost forgotten Tara had gone on that hike but had caught a glimpse of the famous jazz singer in her shorts, tank, and sneakers that were definitely not made for hiking the trails around here.

Viv and Gabe had had a good laugh about the city girl taking on the mountain. Poor thing. And she'd been such a good sport about singing at the last minute when the band canceled. With everything she'd been going through at the time, she'd come through for them.

Viv pushed thoughts of Tara out of her mind. Thinking about her friends put her deeper into her fog of self-loathing and regret. Tara was another friend Viv had ignored. Gabe at least made an effort to keep in touch with many of them. He'd give her updates while she picked at her dinner or mindlessly flipped channels.

She didn't understand how he managed. She needed him just to get through the day, but he didn't need anyone. He certainly didn't need her.

No one did anymore.

She missed being needed.

When they got home, she'd do better. She'd been useful once—she could be again. She'd prove to Gabe how much she cared about him.

And Agnes's ghost could go to hell.

♥♥♥

Gabe's aunt wasn't hard to find. They found her and Albert at the bar. Albert had a drink in his hand, but looked like he hadn't taken a sip. He stared off into space. Agnes kept up a steady stream of chatter with the pretty bartender, but kept her eye on her husband, a small frown on her face.

Albert had already begun slipping by this time. His dementia had gotten worse over the years, to the point where he wasn't able to recognize anyone. Not even Agnes. The poor woman's heart had about broken when that happened. She hadn't lived long after his memory of her completely faded.

Yet once she was gone, Albert hadn't had the will to live on without her. Viv figured a part of him had always known Agnes, though his mind hadn't. No matter how agitated he'd become, Agnes's voice had had the power to soothe him. Without her to hold him to this world, he'd simply slipped away.

Viv wiped a tear from the corner of her eye. She may not have gotten along with Agnes all that well, but she'd always admired her dedication to her husband. And grieved over the way they'd slipped away from each other, though they'd remained together till the end.

Was that where she and Gabe were headed? Together physically, but mentally adrift from each other? The thought terrified her. She felt the color drain from her face. She pressed her palms against her thighs to still the shaking of her fingers.

Gabe strode toward the bar.

"Jimmy. There you are, dear boy." Agnes held out a hand to Gabe. "Albert, Jimmy's here. Make room."

Albert started, spilling some of his beer onto the counter. "Damn it, Agnes. Look what you did. You can't go yelling at a man like that. Near popped my heart right out my chest."

"All I did was talk to you." Agnes's smile was pinched, like she had to force the pleasant expression onto her face.

"That's what I'm saying. Don't do that."

Gabe grabbed the old man's arm when he made to get off his stool. "No worries, Albert. We just wanted to borrow your lovely wife. You mind?"

"Mind?" Albert cackled. "Delighted. Keep her as long as you want. Then maybe a man can get a drink in peace around here. Talk up the ladies." He gave the bartender a lewd wink. She returned the look with a wink of her own.

"Peace would drive you crazy, you old bat." Agnes patted Albert on the shoulder, then slid off her stool. Before leaving, she waved to the bartender. "You let me know if he causes you any problems, all right?"

The bartender nodded. Viv got the feeling Agnes had already made arrangements with her regarding babysitting duties for Albert.

"Lovely." Agnes slipped her arm through Gabe's. "Let's find a nice quiet place to talk, shall we?" She crooked a finger at Viv. "Come along, dear. Don't want you to think I'm stealing your man from you."

Viv barely managed not to roll her eyes as she followed them out of the bar.

♥♥♥

Finding a quiet spot was easier said than done. They ended up under an umbrella, poolside. People milled about, some lay out in the sun, a few braved the pool. Viv had dipped her toe in earlier, surprised at the warmth of the water. She hadn't realized it was heated.

Agnes greeted just about everyone they saw. Viv fluffed her long bangs forward and dipped her chin whenever anyone came near. With oversized sunglasses covering half her face, she hoped that at fifteen years older, with her hair cut short in the back and long in the front, she wouldn't attract anyone's attention with her resemblance to her younger self.

Not so simple for Gabe. Everyone did a double take when they saw him. The gray hair and crow's-feet notwithstanding, he looked the same. Viv was glad they had the ready explanation of a long-lost relative, but it took forever to get somewhere they could talk without an audience. Finally, Gabe told his aunt they really needed to speak to her alone, and she started shooing people away when they looked like they might approach.

Viv didn't hold out hope Agnes would be much help. Gabe tried to get her around to talking about her Wiccan background, but every time he came close, she'd go off on some tangent. She came off as absentminded, but Viv wondered whether she was deliberately avoiding the subject. Agnes was too shrewd. Did she suspect the truth?

"Just spit it out, Gabe." Viv finally lost her temper. The rehearsal dinner was going to start soon and Agnes would end up evading them altogether by claiming she needed to get to the event. Now or never. "Agnes, what do you know about time travel?"

Agnes laughed. "I love time travel. Why, my very favorite book involves a time-traveling nurse." She glanced left and right before leaning forward and whispering, "There's quite a lot of sex in her books, too. Keeps the old heart thumping."

Gabe groaned. "I did not need to hear that."

Viv shot him a dirty look and swatted his arm. "A little less fictional and more practical knowledge, Agnes. You're a witch—how would you make someone travel through time?" A nerve twitched in Viv's temple. What if Agnes figured out what happened and decided not to help them? She didn't approve of the marriage, so why would she help keep Viv and Gabe together?

"Don't be ridiculous, dear. I'm no more a witch than you are. And time travel only happens in stories." Agnes put her hand on top of Viv's. "Are you feeling all right, dear? Maybe you were out in the sun a bit too much today?"

Viv slipped her hand out from under Agnes's, teeth clenched at the all-too-familiar patronizing tone. Agnes had used it with Viv for years—insults veiled in fake concern. If she didn't need answers…

She'd never had the courage to fight back when she and Gabe were dating and then when they were newlyweds. That had come later. Funny…Agnes's grudging acceptance had come shortly after Viv started giving as good as she got.

Before she could think of a suitable response, a bee landed on her arm. She smacked it into her wrist, feeling the sting, but not caring. Damn, she hated the things.

Agnes pushed back in her chair. "Careful, dear. Bee stings can be deadly." Her voice droned on but Viv didn't listen.

Her stomach dropped. A sharp pain pierced her

heart. She was thrown back to the last hike she'd taken with Connor.

They'd loved walking along the nature trails near their home and went out practically every day. Connor picked up every rock, inspected every leaf. He was fascinated by bugs and nature.

They'd never had a problem on their walks. He'd never been stung before. She'd had no way of knowing…

"…runs in the family."

Wait. What?

"My poor brother died from a bee sting."

No. Not possible. She must be hearing things. A knot twisted tight in her stomach.

"No." Gabe sounded as horrified as she felt. "My grand—uh, uncle died of a heart attack."

Agnes shook her head. "No, dear. It was the bee sting that killed him. Someone should have told you." She made a *tsk, tsk* noise. "I'm so glad you've come this weekend. You should have yourself tested. And your kids when you have them. There's things can be done for allergies nowadays that weren't available back then. If you're prepared."

Viv's heart raced. She choked back the scream rising in her throat.

Why? Why didn't anyone tell her?

Her whole body shook.

She should have been told. Someone should have told her.

Air. She needed air.

She could have stopped it. If she'd known, she could have saved him.

"Oh my God." Gabe dropped his head into his hands. "I didn't know. Why the hell didn't anyone ever tell me? Mom said he had a heart attack. No one ever mentioned allergies. Shit."

He continued to curse as Agnes stared at him. Her eyes were wide, her mouth hanging open.

His agony pierced the chaos in Viv's head. She sent her chair crashing to the ground. "Why didn't you ever tell anyone? Why didn't someone tell us?"

Gabe reached for her, but she'd already backed out of range.

The pain in her chest overwhelmed her. She turned away. "I can't—I have to—I need to go."

She took off running. Gabe called after her, but she didn't respond. People were everywhere. Panic fueled her flight. She ignored the stitch in her side as long as she could.

She finally came to a panting standstill near the gazebo. Her mind refused to work properly.

She kept reliving that horrible day in her mind.

And picturing what could have been if she'd been prepared.

She should have been. Why the hell hadn't anyone ever told her? Connor could have gone through allergy testing. If she'd known, she would have kept an EpiPen on her. Given him one and taught him how to use it. She was a teacher so she knew how to use the damn things. Had, in fact, used it in one of her classes once when a student went into anaphylactic shock.

But when her six-year-old son was stung by a bee, she'd been completely ill-equipped. Nine-one-one hadn't been able to reach them in time. They'd hiked too far along the path away from the road.

She'd carried him. Raced to the parking lot, trying to meet them halfway. Felt him slip away from her while they waited for the ambulance.

She'd held her baby while he died. He'd been so scared. She'd told him he'd be okay.

And she'd failed him.

♥♥♥

Viv must have laid still on the gazebo bench for an hour before Gabe came to her. He didn't call her name, stomp his way, or make his presence known in any way. She felt his approach in the tight knot of her stomach, the stiffening of her spine at his scent on the soft June breeze.

He picked up her legs so he could sit with them in his lap. After flicking her shoes off one by one, he massaged her feet in a gentle rhythm. Any other time, she might have enjoyed it.

Instead, she swung to a sitting position, drawing her knees under her chin and wrapping her arms around herself.

"This doesn't change anything," he said. "If we'd known, what would we have done different?"

Her spine hit the gazebo wall as she rocked back and forth. "I might have worried. Had him checked. Carried an EpiPen."

"Doubtful. We'd have mentioned it to his doctor and she'd have told us allergies aren't hereditary."

"How do you do that? Why aren't you freaking out? For the past two years, I've been waiting. Waiting for you to show some goddamn loss of control. Anything. But you've been fine."

"I've been fine?" His voice was colder than she'd ever heard.

She cringed. Why had she opened her stupid mouth?

"Fine?" He jumped out of his seat. Spit out his gum. "What the fuck, Viv? You think I've been fine? I'm so far from fine, it's…" He stomped to a halt and turned to face her.

She shrank away from him. Wished she could pull

her words out of the air as if she'd never said a thing. She'd been thinking it for some time, but the anguish in his eyes proved she'd been beyond wrong. He tore at his hair like he would pull it out at the roots.

She reached a hand out to him, but pulled it back and tucked both hands under her arms. "I didn't mean to imply you don't care. He was the world to both of us. I know that."

"That's good, because I'd leave right now if I thought you believed…" Tears leaked down his cheeks, caught in the rough five o'clock shadow along his jaw. "How can you think I'm fine? How? I wake up in the morning and for a split second I can't remember why my chest feels all tight and I can't breathe. I wait for him to charge into the room and jump on me. And I feel like I'm dying when I realize what's wrong." He clutched at his chest.

"I drive five miles out of my way every day so I don't have to go by the playground and see all those healthy kids running around, playing as if the world has moved on. And it has, but we haven't." He cleared his throat, ran a hand over his bloodshot eyes. "I'm not fine. I'm falling apart. The only thing keeping me going is taking care of you, and I'm doing a piss-poor job of that."

"No." She shook her head. What was he thinking? "You always take such good care of me. And I don't deserve it." She buried her face in her hands, her tears warm against her palms, salty against her lips. "I should have been able to save him," she whispered, half hoping he wouldn't hear. She'd never been able to admit it out loud.

He sighed. "It wasn't your fault."

"You weren't there. You don't know. I promised him everything would be okay." Her voice broke on *okay*.

"Shit. You think I don't regret that every day? I

wasn't there. My son died, and I wasn't there. It was my job to take care of you both. And I failed."

Thump.

She took her hands away from her face. Gabe sat in a heap on the floor, his shoulders shaking with his sobs.

She knelt at his side. Wrapped her arms around his shoulders. "Oh, God no, Gabe. It wasn't your fault."

She recognized the words as the truth. And if they were true for him, were they true for her?

He turned to her and wrapped his arms around her. Buried his head against her chest and sobbed like a child. Tears soaked through her blouse, hot and wet against her skin. He'd been so strong. For her. And she'd been so wrapped up in her own grief, she hadn't realized how much his strength had cost him.

She held him close. It was all she could do as he wore himself out. His shoulders gradually stopped shaking and she noticed the pleasant smell of his aftershave, the warmth of his arms around her. The night breeze was just a little cool against her cheeks. Enough to dry her tears.

His hair tickled her lips as she kissed him on the top of his head. Her frozen heart warmed and the piece of her that belonged to Gabe swelled with love and grief that she hadn't been there for him when he needed her most.

"Oh, Gabe." Tears clogged her voice. She had to clear her throat to get the words out. "I'm so sorry I haven't been there for you."

He raised his head and they came face-to-face, the tips of their noses brushing, almost too close for her eyes to focus properly. But she could see love in his gaze. A love she returned wholeheartedly. They'd lost so much already and come so close to losing each other. She couldn't let that happen.

"I love you," she whispered.

His hand cradled the back of her neck. He placed a ghost of a kiss against her lips. "I love you, too."

♥♥♥

Viv and Gabe sat in the corner of the last row of the large grouping of chairs before the gazebo. All the guests had been ushered to their seats. The groom stood proudly to one side of the minister, waiting for the processional to start.

Up at the front, someone finally hushed Aunt Agnes and Uncle Albert. Viv couldn't hear what they'd been going on about, but they'd certainly involved a number of people, the groom included. He shot them one last venomous glare before shifting his focus toward the inn, where the bridesmaids could be seen coming down the path.

"This is surreal," she whispered.

Gabe had been watching the argument with a confused frown on his face, but now he returned his attention to her.

She nodded toward the approaching processional. "We're about to watch our own wedding from the cheap seats."

He laughed. "Wouldn't want to freak out our younger selves by sitting in the front row." He grabbed her hand and leaned close so their shoulders touched, their hands intertwined in their laps.

"Good point." She watched the bridesmaids in their floor-length purple-and-dove-gray gowns walk down the aisle while Tara played a slow song on the small piano the inn had rented for their wedding. The song ended after

Viv's maid of honor reached the foot of the gazebo.

Tara started to sing "It Was You," the song Nikki had written that weekend. A hush fell over the guests. Everyone stared—not at the bride, but at Tara tucked away in the shadows of the gazebo behind the wedding party.

No one knew the significance of that song until much later. It would become a huge hit.

"It was you who made me see,
"The beginning of a new me."

"I'd forgotten how beautiful her voice is. It's been so long since I listened to one of her albums." Viv turned her attention to her younger self standing at the edge of the white silk runner. The bouquet trembled with the shake of her hands. The bride scanned the backs of all those heads, then focused on the groom, seeking reassurance she'd chosen the right dress. No one noticed. They were all transfixed by Tara's singing.

"I didn't know back then that it would never end.
"I only wanted to love you and have you next to me."

Well, not everyone. Young Gabe had eyes only for young Viv. God, she hoped he'd get that look back in his eyes someday. That she hadn't screwed things up too badly and there was still time to save them.

"You showed me what I never knew.
"And that was to spend my life with you."

She turned to her husband. Her breath released in a gasp.

There was that look. His entire body seemed tuned in to her and her alone. He drank her in with his gaze, like he couldn't get enough of her. She felt beautiful. Wanted.

The only woman in the world.

She couldn't take her gaze off him as Zack began the ceremony.

"Genevieve Allison Bowen, do you take this man, Gabriel Martin Ganivet, as your lawful wedded husband, to have and to hold from this day forward, for better or for worse, for richer or for poorer, in sickness and in health, to love and honor, forsaking all others, till death do you part?"

She stared deep into Gabe's eyes and answered, "I do."

Soft laughter floated on the breeze. She felt it in her bones more than heard it with her ears. As their younger selves exchanged rings, she searched the area for the source.

A ghostly figure stood off in the distance, her face alight with merriment.

Agnes's ghost lifted her hand.

And waved good-bye.

Gabe's hand spasmed around Viv's. She tried to return the pressure, but her strength failed her. The beautiful June sunlight dimmed as if a massive cloud had passed overhead.

She glanced up—not a cloud to be seen.

Sounds receded. The perfume of the roses faded.

Everything went black.

♥♥♥

Viv held a hand to her head, trying to quell the dizziness that made her want to vomit. Her body slowly righted itself and she forced her eyes open.

The soft folds of a dusky rose comforter cushioned her cheek. Something black lay an inch in front of her nose.

She pushed herself off the bed. They were back in their room. Just not the same room she'd been in right before the wedding. The old room's blanket had been a pale blue; this was pink. The black thing that had blocked her vision was her open suitcase.

But she hadn't had a suitcase.

"We're back," Gabe said behind her, a moment before his arm wrapped around her midsection. He pulled her close, burying his face in the crook of her neck.

She settled into his arms. *God, that feels good.* Sadness weighed heavily upon her heart, but there was a light spot where Gabe lived.

"Mom? I'm hungry. Can I order chocolate chip pancakes?"

She must be hearing things. Her heartbeat tripled its pace. The soft chimes of a video game played repeatedly in the background.

Please. Please let it be him.

"Connor?" Gabe's voice broke midway through their son's name.

Their heads swiveled as one to stare at the eight-year-old boy curled up in an armchair in the corner of the room, a game system dangling from his hand.

Memories flooded through her.

Side by side with memories of the past two years after her son's death, were memories of his life.

The first new memory was of Gabe describing Great-Aunt Agnes's scene at the wedding. She'd been talking crazy about time travel and bee stings. He hadn't understood half of what she said, but in the midst of her ranting, he'd learned that his grandfather had died of an allergy, not a heart attack.

The story stuck with Viv, who'd decided to have their baby tested. The bee allergy had been revealed safely in the doctor's office.

In her new memories, she'd had an EpiPen in her backpack when their son was stung while out on a hike. They called it their near miss and while the thought of what could have been scared Viv half to death, Connor had come out of it just fine.

Her limbs refused to move as she absorbed all the new information. Gabe ran to Connor and lifted him in his arms for a bear hug. Connor laughed in delight as his father swung him in a circle, legs swinging wide, head thrown back, his laughter swelling her heart with joy.

Tears streamed down her cheeks. She covered her mouth to stifle her cries. How could she explain to Connor that her tears were of joy at seeing him? He had no idea what they'd gone through.

Thank God.

Gabe stopped swinging and cradled Connor against his chest. He brought his tear-filled gaze up and their eyes locked. He looked as shocked and joyful as she felt.

She rushed into his embrace, their son cuddled between them.

They came together for a kiss over Connor's head.

"Eww!" Connor exclaimed and wiggled until they had to put him down or risk dropping him.

Gabe pulled her closer and they watched their son jump back into the chair with his game. She rested her head on Gabe's chest and sighed in contentment.

Agnes's laughter echoed in her ears. Out of the corners of her eyes, Viv caught sight of the old woman's ghost—a beaming smile lit her face as she nodded to Viv.

Viv whispered, "Thank you."

"Time to go, you nosy old witch," Albert said, appearing beside his wife and slinging an arm around her waist. Viv's eyes widened as the two grew younger. Their spines straightened, gray hair gave way to glossy brown, and wrinkles disappeared. Their love for each other was clear as they looked into each other's eyes. In the midst of a passionate kiss, they faded from sight.

About…

Emma Kaye is married to her high school sweetheart and has two beautiful kids that she spends an insane amount of time driving around central New Jersey. Before ballet classes and tennis entered her life, she decided to try writing one of those romances she loved to read and discovered a new passion. She has been writing ever since. Add in a hyper dog and an extremely patient cat and she's living her own happily ever after while making her characters work hard to reach theirs.

For more information on Emma, please visit her online at www.emma-kaye.com, on Facebook at www.facebook.com/emmakayewrites, on Twitter at www.twitter.com/emmakayewrites or on GoodReads at www.goodreads.com/emma-kaye.

Love time travel? Try another Emma Kaye time travel story—*Time for Love* (finalist in the 2014 Golden Leaf contest.)

♥♥♥

Time for Love

Alexandra Turner will do anything to save her twin sister. Even when she's transported back in time to Regency England. Rescuing her sister and finding her way back to her own time will take all her concentration. Falling in love is not an option.

With the death of his brother, Nicholas Somerville became the ninth Marquess of Oakleigh and must return to England to take his place in society. Part of his responsibility will be to find a wife. It never occurs to him he might actually discover a woman he could love—until he meets Alex on his voyage home.

Can Alex and Nicholas find a way to bridge the gap of time and circumstance? Can they overcome their fears to realize that true love transcends time? Or will a dark secret from Alex's past rear up to separate them forever?

♥♥♥

From This Day Forward

Nicole S. Patrick

♥♥♥

Grammy Award winner Tara Graham's career had hit a high note—until a compromising situation puts her reputation in a bad light. An invitation to a college friend's wedding weekend in the backwoods of Maine is the perfect place to lay low until the bad publicity dies down and her career gets back on track. When a college crush sends her senses into overdrive, will she realize that what she's striving for may not be what she wants, after all?

Former Marine Todd Mitchell's trust in women is jaded. He's grieving the death of his twin brother killed in combat, and trying to rebuild his life in Maine at The Loon Lake Inn. When a beautiful college acquaintance comes to town, he's faced with either opening his mind and heart, or shutting out someone who might be what he needs to learn to trust again.

♥♥♥

Dedicated to ~

My partners, my friends, and my extended family – The Scribes.

Joe, Patrick, and Sean, always.

Mom and Dad, the real-life inspiration behind Agnes and Albert. Your love for each other is truly timeless.

From This Day Forward
by Nicole S. Patrick

Tara Graham cracked one eye at the sound of her ringtone. She glanced at the digital clock—7:00 a.m.?

She reached toward the nightstand, grabbed the phone off the top, and touched the screen. "Did someone die?"

"How drunk were you last night?"

Ron was a terrific agent, but sometimes his timing stunk. "You do realize I was asleep," she croaked. Swallowing proved painful.

"Mmm-hmm…that's what I thought." He huffed. "*Gossip Central* put a story and pictures of you and Ben Pratt on their shitty website. He's holding you against him. Very. Closely. Against him." Ron emphasized the words for dramatic effect, but it only caused throbbing behind her eyeballs. "Oh, darling, that isn't the worst part. There's one of you falling into his limo with your skirt hiked up. Ahem…thank God you had the sense to wear panties. Go look."

Oh no. She wanted to die. When had those paparazzi followed them?

"Reading, brain function—not possible." That champagne and those three—or was it four?—sweet shots hadn't been her wisest choice. Celebrating her Grammy Award with mega movie star Ben—one of her best friends from their grad school days at Juilliard—*had* seemed like a fun idea last night.

"Here's the quote." Ron cleared his throat like he was ready to recite Hamlet's death scene. Tara flopped onto her back and held her aching head. "'Is gorgeous Grammy-winner Tara Graham making moves on Hollywood's most happily married man, Ben Pratt?' Ben's comment to *Gossip Central*'s Mary Healy quotes 'Tara and I are collaborating.'"

She groaned out loud. "What was he thinking?" That gossip magazine queen had a talent for twisting the truth.

"What did you do last night, Miss Tara?" Ron asked in a schoolmarm voice.

"Nothing worth that rag, that's for sure." She grimaced, silently berating herself for one, getting drunk, and two, throwing caution to the wind to let loose for the first time in months.

It'd been a long tour.

"We'll have to do damage control for your night of debauchery," Mother Ron admonished. "You *know* how precarious show business is."

Tara slowly sat up against her headboard and moved her beloved kitty Fat Lorenzo off her lap. "Debauchery? Who uses that word, anyway? Relax. I'm not exactly front-page material." Ron was such a worrywart. So what—a few gratuitous underwear pics put on the net. It would be old news by tomorrow…she hoped.

"Yes, my dear, but Ben Pratt is. And you don't want

bad publicity before your first movie shoot. I'll call Lana. I know you and Ben go way back, but if the rags move on this any more, it'll be a hot mess."

Tara rubbed the bridge of her nose. Ron was right. Lana Ashford, publicist extraordinaire, could make it go away.

"I've got another call." Ron put her on hold before Tara could respond. She pushed aside the covers and slowly swung her feet off the bed.

"Eww…" She looked down at her dress from last night. "Oh God." She gagged at her own stench, a combination of tacos and ashtray.

The last things Tara remembered were crawling into Ben's limo and then into bed.

Alone.

Tara had no romantic designs on Ben.

Never had, never would.

She wasn't the Graham involved with Ben Pratt. *Nope*. That Graham was her sister, Janey. Yes, her baby sis, Jane Graham, bookworm, scientist, MIT grad, had landed herself a leading man.

Also crystal clear from last night: Ben confessing Jane was his "soul mate"…over much whiskey. Tara was tempted to roll her eyes at the memory, but it hurt too much. Really? That stuff only existed in song lyrics.

Of course, Ben had sworn her to secrecy about his and Janey's affair.

What a mess.

But she owed Ben. Without his pull in Hollywood, she'd never have been given a second glance. Jazz pianists weren't exactly up there on the popular meter nowadays. And his new movie about a down-and-out singer/musician was right up her alley. That's what the collaboration was…nothing more. "Ben, you're so dead." Making any other kind of innuendo about them in the press had been a bad idea.

"Wonderful," Ron griped when he returned to the line. "Amanda Cleary's publicist is on the line. And she's just as much a witch as her client. Get some coffee and I'll keep you posted."

Tara stripped, threw on a robe, and padded down the hallway to the kitchen to fire up the coffee pot.

Ben's cell went right to voice mail. Better not leave a message. Amanda sometimes checked them, according to Ben. And the last thing she needed was Amanda calling her.

This situation was getting ridiculous. Jane and Ben were wrong. No matter how much of a witch Amanda was, sneaking around behind Amanda's back had to stop.

Ben and Jane might be in love, but Ben needed to deal with his marital status.

And sweet Janey was not going to be ready for the shit storm of show business gossip when he did.

Running clothes on, Tara grabbed her MP3 player and phone. A Sunday-morning run along the West Side Highway would shake this hangover. She'd deal with the tons of neglected mail later. She grabbed her keys off the foyer table next to the pile, but a large, light purple envelope stuck out, catching her eye. She set down her gear and ripped it open.

Wow. Viv and Gabe were getting married. It'd been so long since she'd contacted any of the old college crew, especially with the workload at Juilliard that had followed.

Those two lovebirds had been together forever. A pang of something she couldn't identify hit the pit of Tara's stomach.

Career first, family later had always been her motto.

And love? Wasn't that the big fat question mark in her life?

The wedding was this weekend in Maine. Damn, the RSVP date was last month. No way could she attend. Between the movie shooting next week and salvaging what gigs she didn't have to cancel because of it, she was booked solid.

Tara locked up and pondered a gift to send.

In the lobby she nodded to Marty the doorman and plucked the sunglasses off the usual place on her head, settling them onto her nose as she stepped through the threshold and onto the street.

A mob of people blocked her path. A guy with a zoom-lens camera practically wacked her in the nose. *How rude.*

"Tara, is it true? Are you and Ben Pratt doing the nasty?"

Huh? Frantic clicking penetrated her brain. The sea of people crowded her, pushing against each other and vying for a place in her face. The mixture of heavy perfume and bad breath made her dizzy. It was suffocating.

"Must've been a good night, eh, Tara?" the zoom-lens guy said in a sleazy voice.

"How does it feel to break up Hollywood's first couple?" another voice piped in.

Tara tried backing away, but something—or someone—pressed against her. Did these people have no concept of personal space? "Please move," she said to no one in particular with surprising calm in her voice, although her pulse raced.

"Come on, Tara. No comment this morning?" someone shouted.

She spun at the hand gripping her upper arm, ready to strike out at whoever dared touch her.

"Miss Graham, come with me." Marty planted his other hand firmly in the small of her back, shielding her body with his, and steered her back inside the lobby.

"Damned vultures." His kind eyes were filled with concern. "Are you hurt?"

Her hands were shaking, more from anger than nerves. "No, no. I'm fine."

The enormity of the situation sunk in as the "vultures" pointed their cameras against the lobby windows. What was going on? No one in the media had ever cared about her before.

Jazz musicians led boring lives—or at least *she* did.

"Maybe you'd better go back upstairs until I can get the garbage cleared out." He glared at the door and straightened his pristine white gloves.

"Yeah, I…thanks," she whispered and headed to the elevator in a daze.

Once inside her apartment, Tara locked the door and attached the chain—which she never did—just as her cell vibrated in her shorts.

"Tara, are you sitting down?" Ron sounded anxious.

"Should I be? Ron, what's going on? The paparazzi are camped outside my building."

"I was afraid of this," he muttered gravely. "Honey, the movie studio called. They're going to replace you."

Tara gripped her keys and sunk to the floor as a wave of nausea rose up to her throat. "I don't understand."

"Amanda Cleary is out for blood. She threatened to pull out of her next blockbuster if you and Ben appear in the movie together."

Her mind raced. "Can she actually do that?"

"I'm not entirely sure," he told her. "She thinks she's more famous than Meryl Streep. I've called an attorney. The studio may be in breach of your contract."

Holy shit. "Ben needs to come clean," she blurted and gripped her stomach.

"Oh, honey, are you in love with him?" Ron's tone was sympathetic.

She scoffed. "Of course not. But I am going to kill him." She couldn't tell anyone about Ben and Jane. The last thing she wanted was for her baby sister to be in the line of fire.

"We'll get this straightened out, I promise."

"Thanks. You're the best." She couldn't ask for a better agent than Ron. She slowly rose from the floor.

"But good luck getting Mr. Pretty Boy to do anything," Ron said.

"What do you mean?"

"Apparently, he's trailed after Queen Amanda to Costa Rica or someplace, according to her publicist. They flew out this morning on her private jet."

Her mind reeled. Did Jane know? Ben was going to be double dead when she got in touch with him, the coward.

"Maybe you should lay low for a few days…you know, until this dies down and we can get your contract sorted out. Take a vacation somewhere remote?"

Her eyes drifted to the invitation on the foyer table. "Good idea." Maine was secluded enough.

♥♥♥

Thwack! The hammer slipped, landing smack on his thumb.

"Son of a…" Todd Mitchell bit back a rather colorful curse at the "Tsk" from below. He hooked the tool into his belt and examined his throbbing digit.

"Are you hurt, my dear boy? Come down and let me take a look."

Dear boy? Since she'd arrived at The Loon Lake Inn, Agnes had appointed herself his unofficial grandmother. His own curmudgeon granny never gave him this much attention. Agnes's latching onto him made him twitchy, but he felt obligated to be nice since she was a guest.

She rose from her chair and hobbled onto the platform of the gazebo where she'd been "supervising" the repairs since six this morning. That back order of lighting from Bangor had better get there for the gazebo to be ready in time for the wedding ceremony.

As for Agnes—for a small lady, she sure was bossy.

At least the garden area had shaped up nicely. The owners, Nikki and Nate, could use the business and suggesting the venue to his old college pals Viv and Gabe for their wedding had been easy. Plus, this job at the inn helped supplement his income while he built up his own survival school business and seemed to be working out great, at least for the time being. He didn't mind the manual labor, and Nikki and Nate treated him well.

Todd grinned despite the pain. Agnes was a trip. He had to admit he hadn't felt like smiling in a long time. However, her "help" consisted of constant chatter about the guests arriving for her great-nephew Gabe's wedding. Whom she liked, which women dressed like hookers— he'd like to see that—and all kinds of comments.

Todd's plan had been to get in a few hours of peace and quiet, but it wasn't to be—not with Agnes hovering.

Summer mornings in Maine were the perfect atmosphere to clear his head. Just him, a raft of loons splashing in the lake, and the buzz of the swarms that made this state their home. He liked Maine but the mosquitoes could give the sand fleas in Afghanistan competition and he had the welts all over his forearms and neck to prove it.

Anyplace but on deployment overseas worked fine for him.

He jumped down from the last rung of the ladder as his watch beeped. The bunch of city guys staying at the inn while the barracks-like structure for his school was built should be out of their racks by now—if they weren't nursing hangovers. Wonder how long they'd last in the woods. In the past few months operating TOSS It, Todd's Outdoor Survival School, a few students had impressed him by getting down and dirty learning how to survive in the wild. Yet others expected the "nature guy" to do all the work.

Not going to happen.

His brochure clearly stated the survival training was no walk in the park. He'd modeled the tactics after his training as a Recon Marine. Being a Marine had taught him many things, and the ability to face adversity and pull shit together was most important of all. The guys who'd signed up for the regimen would soon learn the skill, too.

"Poor thing." Agnes clucked like a mother hen, staring at his still-throbbing thumb. "Did you know I served in the Army Nurse Corps back in fifty-three, at the tail end of the Korean War? I was just a baby back then."

He'd bet a week's worth of rations Agnes had to be pushing ninety if she were a day. For some odd reason it didn't bother him to listen to her nostalgia. Her recollections were a whole lot more interesting than when his grandfather forced him to sit and listen to war stories. "Yes, you mentioned it," he told her.

Agnes pulled a tissue from her pocket to dab the minuscule amount of blood pooling on his thumb. "That's where I met my Albert. He was quite dashing in his Army uniform—not so much anymore."

She stopped and examined him like a piece of meat, then flattened her lips. Not many people could make him squirm like Agnes. "You're a devil dog, I hear."

Todd smirked at the nickname for the Marines. "Yes, ma'am."

Agnes rolled her eyes and patted his arm. "In my heyday, the Marines were crazy fellas. Always getting into bar fights—not that I ever went into a bar." She winked and turned to step off the platform. Todd helped her down with a hand under her elbow. "I had a girlfriend who married a Marine, a rather large and intimidating man—like you, dear. I suppose she found that exciting."

She had a point, although he didn't set out to be intimidating, but at six-three, two-twenty it couldn't be helped.

Agnes was a force of nature, and her husband, Albert, mostly let her boss him around, after they bickered incessantly. They were funny to watch.

"Why don't you have a young lady?" Her bluntness made him flinch. "I hear there are lots to choose around here, but watch out for the hussies after that nice sheriff, Drew." She gave him a stern look. "Steer clear of those types of women. They'll give you diseases."

He gathered his tools to avoid her pointed stare. She'd give any drill sergeant a run for their money. Yeah, poor Drew had his hands full with the women around here. Thankfully they "steered clear" of Todd. Must be his sunny personality.

"I'm about done here." Todd tossed the hammer from his belt into his toolbox. Agnes wasn't only a grandmother type, but a huge gossip, too. Gabe had warned him she had the knack for butting into other people's business.

"The gazebo where my great-nephew and Genevieve will have their ceremony is lovely." She gazed around with a sigh and in no hurry to leave.

He had to agree. The Carolina rosebushes Nikki asked him to plant around the gazebo were full bloomed—a pink backdrop to the stark white of the newly painted wood.

Agnes turned to him with a raised brow. "I understand you know my Gabe well?"

"We went to college together," he mumbled, hoping the answer would suffice. He and Danny both did before they enlisted together. A lump formed in his throat. He pushed his brother's memory into a crevice way back in the recesses of his mind. It was better suited there. Otherwise he just might do something stupid like tear up like a baby in front of Agnes.

Agnes regarded him and chewed her lip. "Ah yes, I seem to recall Gabe mentioning something about your twin brother, Daniel."

He closed the toolbox more forcefully than he'd realized and she flinched with a gasp.

"Oh dear. Now I recall. How insensitive of me." She wrung the tissue between her hands and it crumpled into pieces onto the grass.

Aw hell. Now he'd made her feel bad, when she'd performed makeshift first aid on him and everything. But hearing Danny's name was more than he could handle. He forced down the anguish, which throbbed worse than his thumb. "It's fine, Agnes."

A vee formed in her forehead, mixing with the myriad lines on her face. "No it's not. I'm sorry. Gabe said he was a Marine like you, wasn't he?" At his nod, she continued, "How long has he been gone?"

"Six months," he answered quietly. *Six months and twelve days.* "I could use a strong cup of joe. Can I get you something to drink?" Anything to divert more in-depth talking and going places he didn't want to venture.

Agnes patted his hands and smiled. "You're a dear, dear boy to be so kind to a witless old woman." She pushed off from the chair and he helped her stand.

"You don't fool me. You've got more wits than all of us put together."

She placed a hand on his arm. "Try and make time for love. Albert and I bicker, but there's nothing better. It will help you heal."

Todd peered into her wise blue eyes, with their crinkled corners, but couldn't find any words in response. Love? *No thank you.* Look where it had gotten Danny—a cheating wife and a wooden box.

♥♥♥

There was a moose in the middle of the road.

A big, ugly, smelly thing the size of a bus—and it seemed in no hurry to move out of the way in this century. Its prehistoric-like antlers made it appear ancient. Tara honked the horn several times. Maybe it was old *and* deaf?

It turned its backside to the car and…yes…definitely male. *Holy Jesus, look at the size…*

She squeaked as his enormous head swung to face her. Would he charge the car? The compact rental wouldn't stand a chance. Why hadn't she taken the pickup truck when the clerk at the airport rental desk had offered?

And where was the damn inn? Viv had given her specific instructions over the phone, but there was no sign of it. The turnoff from Moose Creek—which should have been a tip-off to the current situation—stated two miles to The Loon Lake Inn.

"Two miles, by whose standards?" she mumbled. Living in New York City hadn't helped her driving abilities on these bumpy back roads, especially in a five-speed. God, she hoped she wasn't lost.

The endless backwoods had nothing but eastern white pines and maple trees lining the narrow roadway. How she identified the varieties of trees was anyone's guess.

Whenever she got in a stressful situation, she recalled the least-relevant things.

Just before her Grammy Awards performance, she'd recited all forty-three presidents in order to the sound guy. He'd thought she was nuts.

Way back in grammar school, Jane did one of her many science fair projects on tree species or something. "Stop it, Tara. Random memories are not helping your current situation."

She was literally in the middle of nowhere, talking to herself, and it wasn't as if she could ask Bullwinkle for directions.

He'd been chomping on disgusting bits of leaves and grass for the past twenty minutes. Tara swallowed hard. Waiting for him to finish his lunch wasn't on her agenda.

Time to take action.

She'd performed at Madison Square Garden without breaking a sweat, for Pete's sake. She could shoo one moose out of her path, right?

"Buck up, Graham," she muttered and cracked her knuckles. Slowly, she rolled down the window and stuck her head out a bit. Getting out of the car was not going to happen. "Mr. Moose…shoo. Move. Go away! I think I hear Mrs. Moose calling."

His ears flattened against his skull. Maybe he could hear, after all? "Go. Adios. Vamoose." She honked again, and this time pressed her hand against the horn for a few long seconds.

He turned around, and a long strand of gooey dirt and twigs hung from his lips. His giant nostrils flared. *Eww...* In the blink of an eye he was headed straight for the car! How in the world could one big lug move so fast?

Frantically, she tried to put the gearshift into Reverse, but her hands were shaking so badly they slipped off the stick. *Whack*! The blow against the front of the car caused her head to jolt forward. Tara squeezed her eyes shut, covered her head, and waited for the next blow. Wouldn't the gossip rags love this: *Grammy Award winner and husband stealer killed by angry moose in backwoods Maine. Did she have it coming?*

Todd slammed on his brakes around the bend in the road. "What in the hell..." A full-grown bull was about to charge a tin can of a car.

The bull's hooves came down on the hood with such force Todd flinched. Inside the vehicle, a lone woman covered her dark hair with both arms. A loud pop followed by the hiss of steam came from the broken radiator under the hood. It must have spooked the animal since he lumbered off into the woods without a backward glance.

Todd inched his truck forward and stopped in back of the car. He grabbed the ten-gauge from the rack, opened his door, and jumped down. Moose usually didn't come back for round two, but if there was a cow with her calves nearby, there might be more trouble.

The lady didn't move.

Aw hell.

The banging stopped. Was the moose gone, or ramping up for another go at her poor bumper? Tara gradually opened her eyes and wiggled her toes. No paralysis. Then she flexed her fingers and let out a breath she'd been holding for what seemed like forever. Nothing broken.

"Ma'am, are you all right?" A muffled voice came from outside the window and she jerked up her head—and immediately regretted the action. A stab of pain hit her neck muscles like they were on fire. Gingerly, she turned her head and squinted out the driver's-side window.

He was tall, with muscles clearly defined on his biceps and chest beneath his black-and-tan clothing. He was also holding a long gun.

One glance at his face and Tara felt the color drain from her own. The only thing visible was a pair of blue-gray eyes under all that dirt and green-and-brown camouflage paint.

He tried the door handle, then pointed to the lock.

Yeah right, like she was going to open the door.

"Your radiator is steaming. You'd better get out."

A peek over the dashboard showed the rental had turned into a mangled mess thanks to that stupid moose. She had no choice. Tara clicked the lock and the man yanked the door with a screech of metal on metal.

"Is it gone?" Her voice came out in a shaky whisper.

"I think so." A deep, rich baritone voice penetrated through the haze of her panic. It was a nice sound. Soothing. The pounding of her heartbeat in her ears started to subside.

He surveyed the woods then propped his gun against what remained of the front bumper.

"Did you shoot it?" she asked, hesitantly.

His eyes swung back to her face and he frowned. "No," he replied like her question was absurd. "It ran off on its own."

He glanced at his watch. Guess he had someplace to be? From the way he examined the rental's front and rear before looking back down the road, Tara felt like she should apologize for being in his way. Maybe he was one of those loner guys who cared about nothing but nature and lived in some decrepit old cabin—like the Unabomber? *Great. A moose, and now some crazy guy in camouflage.*

But when Tara swung her legs outside the open door she didn't mistake his abrupt stop and eyebrow raise at her short sundress as anything but blatant interest.

Her new gold-and-pink high-heeled strappy Jimmy Choo sandals perfectly complemented the off-the-shoulder dress. But next to his serviceable and well-worn clothes she felt like a fish out of water...and practically naked.

Who knew she'd be accosted by a rogue moose on the way to a wedding weekend, for crying out loud. She should've worn combat boots and overalls, not that she owned any.

He reached out a hand to help her, but retracted it quickly to wipe the dirt onto his pant leg. At least he showed some courtesy for a guy who smelled like...what was that smell, anyway? *Don't judge, Tara, he may have just saved your patootie.*

"Moose one, car zero?" She pointed to the wreck with a laugh.

No reaction other than a blink at her lousy attempt at a joke. His eyebrows were dark brown under the edge of the knit skullcap. Wonder if his hair was the same color? With a clenched jaw, he hadn't cracked the slightest hint of a smile. Whoever said Mainers were a friendly bunch was sadly mistaken.

Tara took a step back and landed on a rock under the thin sole of her shoe. Her ankle buckled and she shot out a hand to steady herself at the same time he gripped her elbow. Even with the five-inch heels, he towered over her.

"Um…thanks. I guess it's safe to assume this isn't drivable." Mr. Friendly, here, would have to give her a ride. *Wonderful.* It was the only other option to being stranded in the woods without a car. *Double wonderful.* For the umpteenth time since she'd left New York, she wanted to kill Ben Pratt, who, as it happened, was still MIA.

Mr. Friendly had popped the trunk and retrieved her bags by the time she'd snapped out of her own misery.

"I could've gotten those…" He heaved—literally threw—her set of Louis Vuitton bags over his shoulder and into the dusty bed of his pickup truck. At least there weren't any dead animals keeping her expensive luggage company. Grabbing her handbag and phone charger from the front passenger seat, Tara carefully made her way around the ruts in the road to his truck. "I'm going to The Loon Lake Inn, in case you're wondering."

"Figured." He opened the passenger-side door, then walked around to his side.

Wow, wasn't he the chatterbox?

She reached for the grab handle on the door and hoisted herself into the seat. Her dress rode up her thighs and she caught his glance zero in on the spot. She yanked it down then tried to pull the seat belt across her chest but couldn't manage it. "Ouch." God, that moose had done some type of damage to her neck. It hurt like mad.

Suddenly, his sweaty face appeared right next to hers and she reared back.

"Are you injured?"

Now he asks? He hadn't offered up his name. Guess manners weren't abundant here in Maine, either. "My neck wrenched when Bullwinkle decided to try and punt my rental."

He laughed out loud—the last sound she'd expected to hear—and she turned to face him like a deer in headlights. Pearly white and perfectly straight teeth gleamed against the black of the paint when he smiled and she almost died right there on the spot. He was freaking gorgeous. Damn, even wearing the war paint, he'd put any movie star to shame. Too bad he didn't smell or act as nice as he looked.

"Bullwinkle?" He smirked.

"We didn't exactly exchange names," she mumbled, smoothed out her skirt, and tried to get a grip on her racing pulse and the clench in her stomach muscles.

She nearly jumped out of her own skin when his arm swung over the seat back and his hand grazed her shoulder. Jeez, what was wrong with her? Her nerves were shot.

As he turned to glance over his shoulder and back up the vehicle, his shirt stretched to the limit across his defined abs. The man probably had less than ten percent body fat. Must be all that hunting and traipsing around the woods. He and his cut muscles were a far cry from the skinny musicians she dated on rare occasion. How long had it been since she'd been this close to someone so…male? He positively oozed testosterone.

She cleared her throat to change the direction of those types of thoughts. "What should I do about the car?" Tow trucks were probably not in abundance around here.

"I'll call the sheriff and have it moved," he replied matter-of-factly.

Guess he knew the sheriff?

When he maneuvered around the wreck, his truck dipped into a valley in the road. Without her seat belt attached she lurched to the side. Tara's hand shot out to balance herself and her palm smacked on top of his thigh…a very rock-hard, warm thigh covered in cargo pants.

She snatched her hand away. "Sorry," she mumbled.

He didn't say a word, just kept his eyes on the road. Tara scooted as far away from him as possible. She leaned against the passenger door and considered throwing herself from the vehicle. The tension in the air was stifling. She cracked open her window even though his air conditioner blew full blast.

The late-afternoon sun reflected off the truck's windshield as he drove silently. It seemed like an awful long way to the inn.

Tara reached for her sunglasses atop her head and found nothing. *Damn.* She must've dropped them in the car.

The glare of the sun made her eyes water so she pulled down the visor and a picture fell onto her lap. Two Marines in full dress uniforms smiled at the camera in an easy, laid-back pose. One had his arm around the other's shoulder.

Wait, she knew them.

Todd and Danny Mitchell? The gorgeous twins from college?

Why would Mr. Friendly have a picture of…*no, it couldn't be*. She peered at Mr. Friendly's profile. "Todd?"

"Yeah?" he asked suspiciously, glancing at her for a split second.

Tara almost laughed out loud at the irony. Mr. Friendly equaled none other than Todd Mitchell. No wonder her girlie parts were all tingly. She'd had the worst crush on him back in the day.

And he apparently still brooded as much as he did in college. Not much had changed there, either.

But the rest of him…*wow!*

And, oh no…he probably thought she was just some

airhead in high heels needing rescuing. *Way to make an impression.* She had hoped to appear the cool and successful Tara Graham when she reacquainted with her college friends, not act like the music geek she used to be.

"I'm Tara," she finally said, after wishing the last half hour of her life could be a do-over.

He shrugged one shoulder. "Hi, Tara."

He didn't remember her? Well, that sucked.

"Tara Graham," she tried again, waiting for signs of recognition.

Still nothing.

College wasn't *that* long ago. "We went to college together. I used to be…err…still am friends with Viv and Gabe—which makes sense that you're here, too, since I'm also here for their wedding." *Keep blabbering, Tara, real attractive.* "How's your brother, Danny? He used to throw wild parties back then." She smiled as the memories surfaced. For the first time since she'd gotten into his truck, Tara felt a bit more relaxed.

Except then his whole body tensed and he gripped the steering wheel.

Uh-oh. Her face fell. Had she said something wrong?

He turned the truck at the entrance to The Loon Lake Inn in tense silence. Whatever had crawled up his butt was his problem.

She'd just enjoy the weekend catching up with old friends, and try to be civil to Todd, or better yet, steer clear of him altogether. Looks weren't everything. A good personality, which he hadn't grown much of since college, mattered more than a hot bod.

The sight of the lovely building with its Old World style took her breath away, and she almost forgot about brooding Todd. The large log cabin structure included a glass elevator on the outer wall up to the second story. What a cozy, yet elegant place.

Todd put the truck in Park and opened his door to get out, but then he turned and stared straight into her eyes. The anguish on his face made her suck in a breath.

"Danny's dead." He slammed the door and walked away.

♥♥♥

Todd strode away from his truck in a tunnel-vision haze. He marched through the inn's doors and bypassed guests milling in the lobby with the blood pumping through his system pounding loudly in his head. Someone said hi but he couldn't respond. He knew leaving Tara Graham alone in his truck wasn't the most honorable thing to do, but saying those two simple words—"Danny's dead"—out loud made it hard to breathe. And hyperventilating in front of a drop-dead-gorgeous woman wasn't on his bucket list.

Christ. The grief continued to eat him up inside. How long until it let up? How long until he could say Danny's name without falling apart?

Nikki manned the front desk and glanced up at him with a funny look. "Todd, you okay?"

It didn't help that he sported camo face and smelled like deer piss. "There's a guest in my truck named Tara Graham whose car had a run-in with a bull." He barely made out the words through gritted teeth.

His chest felt like a thousand-pound moose was using it for a couch. Unfortunately, the symptoms weren't foreign. At all. He needed to get back outside, and quick—in nature, with clean oxygen coming from the forest. It was the only place he felt any relief.

Nikki pulled a bottle of water from the fridge next to her desk and handed it to him over the counter. "Drink this and do what you have to do."

And just as suddenly as it had started, the anxiety began to melt away with the first sip then guzzle of water.

Nikki smiled, as if sensing he'd been in the throes of an attack. She was one in a million. "Better?"

He nodded. "Will be. I'm going to walk to my place…don't want to stink up your lobby. Leave the truck—I'll move it later and tell the sheriff. Tara's car needs a tow."

Todd slipped out the door toward the place Nikki had leased to him. An acre of her land with the half-finished log cabin—what would eventually include the office for his school.

Branches crunched under his boots as his heartbeat slowed and he considered Tara Graham. She'd changed so much he hadn't recognized her. No more glasses and rock band T-shirts. That dress and shoes…*wow*. His mouth dried thinking about her long, tan legs in those sandals. The bull didn't know what he'd missed when he'd hightailed it into the woods.

She hadn't recognized him off the bat, either. Probably due to his face paint and her round with Bullwinkle. He chuckled silently at the name.

Funny, just thinking about her sexy bare shoulder in that outfit counteracted the aftereffect of his panic attack. He let out a long breath. *Aw hell*, he'd have to explain his actions to Tara, or least try to later when he had his head back in the game. The wedding weekend would uncover if he were fit for civilized conversation again. Most of the time he made do with smelly guys traipsing in the woods. He was mighty rusty when it came to talking to a beautiful woman.

Danny had always wanted to hook up with Tara, but

for some reason they never had. His brother sure would've been better off with a person like her, instead of his lying, cheating wife, Marissa.

Danny's dead? Disbelief hit the pit of her stomach and Tara tried to process what Todd had said, but all she could do was stare out the windshield.

Then her door swung open and Viv pulled her out of the truck and into a big hug. Gabe stood nearby.

"We're so thrilled you could make it." Viv's arms tightened around Tara's shoulders.

Viv hadn't changed. She was still the same bubbly, happy person she'd been in college.

The bride-to-be herded Tara into the lobby, relaying who had arrived and the activities planned. All throughout, Tara's head spun.

"Wait." Tara turned back to the door. "My luggage—"

"Don't worry." Gabe waved his hand. "I'll have someone bring in your bags."

Would have been nice if Todd had done it. How could he just drop a bombshell like Danny dying and disappear?

Rattled to the core, Tara approached the check-in desk and tried to focus as Viv introduced her to a lovely woman named Nikki. Tara managed to pay attention enough to learn Nikki and her husband Nate owned the inn.

Nikki smiled with a warm welcome.

"Um…my rental car is badly damaged. I had a moose incident." Tara shook her head in disbelief, not wanting to relive the past half hour. "I never thought in a million years I'd get to use *I* and *moose* in the same sentence."

Nikki's eyes dimmed with sympathy. "I'm sorry you were introduced to The Loon Lake Inn by a disaster, Miss Graham. Todd already filled me in. Are you okay?"

Tara cleared her throat as Nikki handed her a room key. "I'll be fine. Is Todd still around? I never got to properly thank him…" Her voice trailed off as Nikki tilted her head and peered at her curiously.

"He said he had a few things to take care of."

"Oh, I see." Tara bit her lip and nodded. Guess he'd found the courtesy to tell Nikki he had "things to take care of."

Tara swallowed a lump of anger rising in the back of her throat. Why were his actions still bothering her? So what if Todd didn't remember her? He couldn't be expected to match her now twenty-pound-lighter body clad in a much better wardrobe than a girl from college. But to drop her off like a stray—talk about downright rude.

Men with no consideration were getting on her last nerve.

"Enjoy your stay," Nikki said with a smile.

"What room are you in?" Viv asked.

Tara checked her key. "Two-eighteen."

"It's not far. I'll show you." Viv pointed to the elevator.

"Great." Tara fell in step behind.

"Get settled and I'll buzz you later," Viv instructed. "There's an itinerary in your room. There's lots of stuff planned for our guests. Right, honey?" Viv motioned for Gabe, who was conversing with another guest.

Itinerary? Tara hoped to lay low and relax until the wedding. "Sounds like fun," she murmured, wanting to ask Viv about Danny, but knowing it'd be a buzz kill.

"Need to finalize the musicians," Gabe informed Viv. "See you later, Tara." He walked away as the elevator opened.

Tara admired the view on the way up. Through the floor-to-ceiling glass, acres of green and gold trees and tons of purple lilac bushes surrounding the lake showed their magnificence.

They exited and Viv pointed out the direction of her room. "I'm glad you fit our wedding into your busy schedule, being a famous star and everything." Viv winked.

"Oh please, I'm hardly that." If only Viv knew what a failure she felt like. *Star?* Yeah, sure, a star without a movie. Thanks to a hidden clause in her contract she'd indeed been canned. And the gigs she'd canceled were already rebooked. *So much for moving up in my career.*

♥♥♥

Janey wasn't telling her the whole story.

Tara stared at her cell phone after hanging up with her sister and bit back a curse. She'd bet her best pair of Manolos that Amanda Cleary still had her hooks in Ben and wasn't letting him out of her sight.

Janey, in her usual kind way, suggested Tara enjoy the wedding and that things would work out. How could things possibly work out? It wasn't like Ben was answering his phone. Something was up.

There wasn't much to be done from Maine, but that didn't stop her from worrying. Janey had no clue how horrible the paparazzi vultures could be, especially when the word got out about the affair with Ben.

Tara tossed the cell phone onto the comforter and stretched her arms overhead. That nap and long soak in the oversized tub she'd just enjoyed helped ease the ache in her neck. Never one to be lazy, she had to admit it felt good for a change.

According to the "wedding itinerary" there was some kind of welcome party tonight, then a nature hike tomorrow morning. *Oh joy.* Maybe Mr. Moose would make a guest appearance. The rehearsal tomorrow night, and the wedding ceremony on Saturday, made up the weekend's events. Plus, couples' bingo, shuffleboard, and a host of other activities to choose from.

The few weddings she'd attended were mostly working gigs in her early career, and six-hour affairs at most.

And Ben's wedding technically didn't count. He and Amanda eloped. And lucky her, she had stood in as a witness because she'd just happened to be doing a show at Caesars Palace in Vegas the same weekend.

That marriage was doomed from the start. Ben refused to see it, but Amanda led him around like a marionette on a string. No wonder he'd fallen for Janey and her laid-back, trusting nature.

Try as she might to not think the worst, the more Ben remained incommunicado, the more Tara knew Janey would wind up devastated. And then Ben Pratt would wish he'd never batted his baby blues at her baby sister.

This is why I don't believe in love or relationships. Nothing but one heartache after another. Better to concentrate on success and accomplishments than fleeting feelings.

Tara checked her watch and grabbed her wrap before heading out the door.

She silently padded across the polished wood floor in her ballet flats toward the banquet room. The white capris and canary-yellow sheer wrap over her camisole was fashionable and more comfortable than the heels and Gucci dress she'd had on earlier.

A few guests milled around the lobby and a couple

played chess by the fireplace. Nikki waved from the front desk and Tara acknowledged the greeting, then pretended to study the stack of brochures on area attractions. In reality, she searched the area for Todd. No luck. A pang of disappointment hit her empty stomach.

A familiar tall man stopped by the desk to converse with Nikki. When he turned around, Tara's eyes widened.

Morgan Stuart? The hotshot attorney had sponsored a fund-raiser fiasco she'd recently played. Oh God, how awkward. Her guitar player, Jimmy, had come down with the mumps two days before the show, and the ringer had been awful, not to mention drunk as a skunk. When he'd fallen off the stage, Tara had wanted to die of embarrassment.

Morgan turned and Tara tried stepping away, but he'd spotted her. *Damn.*

Tara smoothed down her hair and readjusted the clip at the nape of her neck. The long curls were unruly after the bath.

"Tara?" With surprise on his face, Morgan approached and gave her a kiss on her cheek. "How have you been?"

Guess there wasn't a way to make a graceful exit without appearing rude. She smiled instead. "Hi, Morgan. I'm fine." At least he hadn't mentioned the fund-raiser. Maybe he'd forgotten. "Are you here on vacation or business?"

"For the wedding," he answered. "I know the groom. And you?"

"Went to college with both Viv and Gabe way back in the day, and no I will not admit how old I am." She smirked and he laughed.

Out of the corner of her eye, Tara noticed an older lady sitting on a brocade chair near the fireplace giving them the stink eye. Morgan tilted his head to the side and pursed his lips. "You up to doing a favor for our friends?"

Favor? "Um…I guess. How so?"

"The band just canceled and Gabe is sweating bullets, trying not to ruin Viv's plans. He wants everything to be perfect for her."

Of course Gabe would do everything in his power to make Viv happy. They were both so much in love. Ugh…there was that word again. Between Viv and Gabe beaming, and Janey pining over Ben, love oozed everywhere.

But the idea of playing their wedding appealed. It'd be a nice throwback to the old days, before all the notoriety nonsense. No paparazzi, no making nice with producers or always feeling like she had to be on her game. Yeah, maybe a simple set of happy wedding music would be a nice change.

"I'd be honored to play." Excitement curled in her stomach. "But can you do *me* a favor?" At his nod she said, "I have some legal questions I'm hoping you can answer about a breach of contract for a movie I should have been shooting next week, which led to me canceling a host of shows. It's a mess."

"Uh-oh. Sounds like there's a story. Let's head to the lounge and talk."

Tara allowed him to lead the way and after tucking themselves into a lounge area she caught him up to speed with everything she knew so far.

After the talk with Morgan, Tara found the way to the party. Buffet tables sat adjacent to the pitted oak door and the DJ urged the guests to fill the dance floor.

Gardenias, lilacs, and wildflowers bloomed in vases placed on tables and in every crevice of the room. Tara caught sight of Davina and enveloped her old friend in a hug. Learning she'd become a doctor and reminiscing helped Tara relax, which was probably why she agreed to do a shot for old times' sake. After choking on the fiery liquid, she excused herself and ordered a seltzer with lime.

She found a seat at a cocktail table and nibbled on boiled shrimp and crackers. The DJ played a mixture of oldies and new pop and she tapped her foot along to the music.

"Jack with ice," said a familiar baritone from the end of the bar.

Her stomach flipped and she blatantly studied her old college crush. Todd still sported the five o'clock shadow from earlier, but on him the scruff worked. He'd washed off the backwoods-hunter look and donned a pair of khakis and a blue collared golf shirt tucked into a belt, showing off his flat abs.

And, Lord, his biceps were the size of her calf muscles.

A hint of an eagle and anchor tattoo showed at the edge of his shirtsleeve and it was sexier than anything she'd ever laid eyes on.

The DJ turned up the music and the dance floor filled with guests swaying to the latest pop hit. Todd casually adjusted his position and surveyed the crowd, giving her a bird's-eye view of his backside. *Wow, did it suddenly get steamy in here?*

She couldn't recall the last time any man had made her tingle all over. She downed her seltzer and promptly choked on a shrimp.

Todd whipped around and spotted her. Grabbing his drink off the bar, his long stride ate up the distance just as she managed to inhale. He plopped his drink on the table but didn't sit, and she was forced to tilt her head back at his height. The motion caused a jolt to her sore neck and she winced.

"Are you still in pain from this afternoon?" His

eyebrows drew down in concern.

She couldn't answer. Words escaped at the feel of his hands massaging the point where her shoulders blades met the curve of her neck. She forgot about why she was mad at him and turned into one big pile of mush.

One of his hands was cold from being around the glass, and the other was scorching hot—a perfect balance for her aching neck.

The feel of him working out the stiff kinks was just too damn enticing to tell him to stop. Again, out of the corner of her eye she spotted that old lady she'd noticed staring at them earlier. How creepy.

Tara cleared her throat and wiggled a little so Todd would get the hint and drop his hands. "That's…um…not necessary, but it helped. Thanks."

He turned the chair around and straddled it, like he didn't have a care in the world for etiquette, just a manly, rugged way about him. The corner of his mouth lifted and he ducked his head. "It's the least I can do for dumping you at the front door earlier. Can we start over?"

"No." She shook her head.

His mouth dropped open for a second and then his lips flattened together.

Maybe she'd better clarify before he went into brood mode again. "I will not go another round with Bullwinkle. No way, no how."

His mouth relaxed and his eyes twinkled. He rubbed a hand over his short hair. And yes, as she'd suspected, the color was mahogany, the same as the eyebrows above his deep blue eyes. "I didn't mean that far back."

"Oh good. You had me worried for a moment," she teased. If he were going to make amends, there was no need to be a bitch. "Sorry, but one moose encounter is enough for a lifetime, thank you very much." She stuck out her hand. "Tara Graham. We attended the same college. It's nice to see you again."

Todd barked out a laugh and shook his head, but not before he bit his bottom lip between his teeth—a swoon-worthy gesture. *Girl parts tingle alert.*

"Todd Mitchell. It's a pleasure to see you, too, Ms. Graham. You look lovely and so different from college." He turned her hand over in his large one and placed a soft kiss on her knuckles and Tara was glad to be sitting. Her knees would have surely given out if not. Such a formal gesture, but the sensations made her feel like they were the only two in the room.

"Mr. Mitchell, I'm not sure how to take that statement, but I'll put it in the compliments column."

"Insert foot in mouth, huh?"

Tara hated to ruin their light banter but she needed to ask about Danny. Her smile fell as she gently pulled her hand away.

Understanding registered in his eyes. "I know," he said quietly in answer to her unspoken question. He took a sip of his drink. "Danny." With his long sigh, it seemed the world had dumped itself onto his broad shoulders. "You want to take a walk in the garden? It's kinda loud in here."

"Sure," she agreed, curious about Danny, but also wanting to ease whatever hurt was going on inside of him. That hard exterior she'd witnessed earlier was gone.

Todd's chest loosened as soon as he opened the patio doors—the silence a welcome change from the pounding music of the ballroom. He directed them through the gardens and toward the gazebo. When his fingers grazed Tara's trim waist at the small of her back, a tinge of heat sliced into his palm. The faint hint of her perfume hit his nose and he couldn't help himself; he leaned closer. The riot of chestnut curls reaching the middle of her back smelled like berries, fresh and sexy at the same time.

He motioned to one of the wooden benches set out for the wedding ceremony.

"Is this where the wedding will be?" she asked, looking around.

He sat next to her. "That's the plan. I need to finish a few things, but a late delivery slowed me down."

"Everything looks good to me." She smiled faintly, yet questions about Danny clearly showed on her face.

His gut clenched. Was he ready to talk?

Their flirting sure helped ease the tight coil of grief winding through his insides like a constant vise. Gabe had mentioned she was some sort of famous award-winning recording star. Not that she acted like it. The few famous people he'd met while traveling the world with the Corps were snotty and aloof.

Todd cleared the lump in his throat. "Danny's been gone a little over six months and it's still really raw for me to talk about."

His breath came out in a whoosh. He'd never uttered those exact words to anyone. It was like admitting his weakness, when all he ever did was hide behind his size and strength.

Maybe it was the way she turned toward him to give him her full attention, or the distress he saw reflected in her eyes that had him confessing. She showed genuine concern, not pity.

"Todd, if I would've known, I'd never have been so flippant. I'm so sorry." Her eyes dropped to her lap.

Guilt hit the pit of his stomach like a brick. *She* was apologizing? Now he felt like more of an ass for his actions. "No, I'm sorry. I shouldn't have bolted on you earlier."

"Can you tell me what happened?"

Her soft words sucked him in and he got lost in her chocolate-colored eyes. Incredibly long lashes framed their depths and he found himself staring at their beauty.

She shifted and he could've smacked himself for allowing the silence to build.

"If you'd rather not, or it's too much, that's fine, too." She bit her lip and he honestly believed she'd given him an out from talking about it.

Oddly, that gave him the strength to continue. He swallowed hard. "Well, we both enlisted in the Marines after senior year ended, which pissed off our parents. Said they'd wasted all that tuition money. But after nine-eleven and the war continuing, Danny and I knew what needed to be done. I'll tell you boot camp was an eye opener for two pampered college boys." He shook his head with a smirk. "Then deployment after deployment happened. We both thought about making the Corps a career."

"That must have been interesting, you know, traveling the world and all."

He shrugged. "The traveling part was okay, but Danny wanted to be home more. He'd gotten married."

Her eyes widened. "Married? That's nice, I guess. Not that I would know."

"Me neither," he admitted. "I got banged up— shot—then discharged. The Corps wouldn't send me on recon missions because of my injury, and I hated the idea of a desk job."

"You don't look injured." She perused his body, chest to boots. "Um…at least to me you don't. But what do I know…go on," she stuttered and fidgeted with the wispy wrap thing around her shoulders.

Tara had a shy air about her, something else he'd never expected from someone famous.

He rubbed the back of his neck and forced himself

to continue. "Danny had one last tour to finish before heading home to be closer to his wife."

The tick in his jaw started to throb as he relived the scenario in his mind. Rage bubbled inside at the memory of Danny's shattered face when his twin discovered the truth…

Tara's knee brushed against his as she shifted on the bench.

"Danny's wife, Marissa, wasn't there when he returned stateside. She was too busy fucking someone else." Despite the fact that he'd never have to lay eyes on that bitch again, Todd's blood boiled at her name.

Tara tensed with a small gasp, but he wouldn't glance at her. No telling what kind of hell she'd have to witness in his eyes at the moment. He had to pull it together. Talking about this out loud might have seemed like a good and cathartic idea, but actually doing it was killing him.

"A week later he volunteered to ship out again. *Volunteered.*" The words came out through gritted teeth. *Stupid…impulsive Danny.* His brother thought he could run away. "I tried talking sense into him. But he was…destroyed. Marissa couldn't deal with him being married to the Corps. She hurled at me how I got hurt and left, and how Danny only stayed in just to please me, which was such *bullshit.*" Marissa always pushed the blame onto someone else's shoulders.

He cleared his constricted throat. *Damn, if the words weren't stuck.* "Two weeks overseas, his platoon was ambushed." His voice cracked in a whisper.

Her soft, anguished moan forced him to focus on her. "Oh no," she whispered.

And here came the hardest part of all—the guilt chapter.

"You see, I wanted to warn him so many times about her. I suspected she was cheating, but had no real proof so how could I hurt him like that? Hell, I'd introduced them. Stupid, huh?"

Tara's body tensed at his words and her brows creased. "Danny merely wanted to love her, and she stepped all over him. I can't stand people like that."

He had the feeling Tara wasn't talking about Danny with that statement.

Then she surprised him by grabbing both his hands, with a strong grip for a slight person. "I know I shouldn't be so mean…but what a bitch."

"You're absolutely right, she is."

Her sexy lips flattened and there were unshed tears in her eyes. That Tara was angry loosened the vise in his chest a notch. Someone who shared the combination of grief and anger he grappled with whenever he thought about his ex-sister-in-law helped so much. Marissa had lost a husband, but she'd never deserved Danny in the first place.

"I'm sorry you lost Danny. He was a great guy who deserved better," she said, as if reading his thoughts.

As he soaked in her breathtaking face, he silently berated himself for missing out on Tara Graham. Why hadn't he given her a second glance in college? Was it because of Danny? She'd always been super friendly. But at the time he'd been a jock and she into music. Must've seemed like a good reason back then. But now? She wasn't wearing a wedding ring, and she'd come alone. Nothing to stop him…

His brother's voice seeped into his head, which happened often lately. *Go for it, idiot. She's hot and she's feeling you, bro.*

So Todd did the first thing that made sense in a long time.

He kissed Tara.

Todd gently grasped the back of her head and pulled her toward him in a very alpha-male, possessive, and freaking exciting way. She'd felt their connection as he spoke of Danny, but certainly didn't expect this.

He took charge and slanted his lips across hers. Strong, yet soft lips caressed hers. He tasted like whiskey, and at the first stroke of his tongue, she was jelly all over. He tugged away the clip in her hair and wound his fingers through her tangled curls. *Girlie parts overload.*

She gripped his biceps and sucked in a breath at the sheer strength beneath her fingertips. He deepened the kiss and one of his hands slid down to her waist.

It had been forever since she'd felt any man's lips against hers, and his were delicious. She wanted to jump into the moment headfirst, no holds barred. But wait…this was nuts. He'd poured his heart out and the last thing she wanted to be accused of was taking advantage of his grief.

Tara broke the kiss first—if not, she might do something impulsive like drag him to her room and strip him of his khakis in a heartbeat. *Grammy winner shags distraught Marine. Is she at it again?*

Headlines be damned. She needed to stop worrying about it. If anyone thought the worst of her, so be it. As long as Janey stayed protected.

But Todd deserved to know the crazy stuff going on—or not going on—in her screwed-up life if they were going to… *Forget it, Tara.* Laying low was the plan for this trip, not getting laid. *Girlie parts disappointed.*

She flattened her hand on the warm wall of his chest and the staccato heartbeat under her palm matched her own rapid pulse. "Wow."

"Tell me about it." He smiled—actually smiled—and Tara almost second-guessed her decision. Her clip had fallen somewhere on the grass in the throes of their kiss, and her wrap pooled around her waist. She tugged it up to her shoulders as he pushed a lock of hair behind her ear. The gentle gesture coming from such a hard man made her breath hitch. Bet he'd be gentle in other ways, too. *Settle down, girlie parts…no is no.*

"Thank you for telling me about Danny. It couldn't have been easy for you." She stood and he did the same.

His eyes searched her face and he leaned in and gave her a gentle kiss. Nothing half as steamy as before but just as unsettling. *Don't think too much into this.* In the heat of the moment, strange things happened. Better to think that than to try and decode the warmth inside of her chest.

Then he gave her hand a gentle squeeze. "Thanks for listening. You're easy to talk to."

"My pleasure." He seemed more at ease, and she was happy to have helped him. "I'd better head in. It's an early day tomorrow, according to the itinerary." Time to exit stage left or succumb to the things she *really* wanted to do with him.

♥♥♥

"…want to welcome you all to the nature hike," said a voice from the front of the crowd.

Finally, she'd located the group assembled at the edge of the woods behind the pool. Her takeaway coffee cup firmly in hand, she smiled politely to the other guests and groaned inside.

Was everyone around here the poster child for outdoorsman? Had she missed something on the itinerary about gear?

Everyone had canteens around their necks and

sported the Indiana Jones look.

Her running shorts, tank, and old pair of running sneakers would have to do. The others had on hiking boots, backpacks, and hats. Damn…she'd forgotten to pack a ball cap to ward off the sun.

A buzz whizzed past her ear and she nearly spilled the coffee down the front of her white tank. *Great. Bugs.* This was a far cry from Central Park.

"For any latecomers needing a canteen and repellant, please come up." She knew that voice—or her body did. Tingles started around her midsection, then dipped lower. Memories of that scorching kiss she tried to forget last night surfaced.

"Don't be shy. I've got plenty."

No one moved or seemed to need gear. How had Todd noticed her way in the back? Might as well do what he asked.

Tara weaved through the crowd to where he was bent over, pulling stuff from a large canvas duffel stamped with the US Marine Corps logo.

He rose and the tingles increased as his eyes traced up her legs, past her torso and then to her face. "Good morning, Ms. Graham."

"Morning," she murmured, suddenly feeling shy. She was never on her game before caffeine kicked in.

"Do you have hiking boots?" At her head shake, he sighed. "Be careful where you step. Those shoes have soft soles." He handed her a full canteen, its strap dangling from his fingers, and before she had time to thank him a cold blast of bug spray hit her legs.

Then he spun her around to administer the foul-smelling mist in a long spray to the backs of her arms.

"Hey…what?" She jumped, keeping a death grip on her coffee.

Todd leaned in close so no one else could hear.

"You smell amazing to me, but the bugs will think you're breakfast." Then he winked and Tara thought she'd imagined it because his face went back to being all-serious.

Smell amazing? She didn't know what to make of this flirty Todd.

Two hours later, and a few hundred thousand bug swats despite the repellent, Tara came to the conclusion nature wasn't her thing. Todd, on the other hand, was an amazing guide, patiently answering questions. More than a few of the ladies stared at his back end as they marched through the brush. She couldn't blame them—it was a work of art.

She'd stuck to the back of the group, not asking questions, nor standing out. But luckily someone asked what else he taught. His school on the property taught survival skills. No surprise there. Todd handled the outdoors with ease. He explained various edible plants—not that she'd ever sample any—and types of animal tracks to be aware of.

While the others snapped photos of plant life and took a water break, Tara sat on a thick log and gazed at Loon Lake.

What a peaceful place—the opposite of the hustle and the bustle of the city, recording studios, and drama. She felt like a normal everyday person again without worry about contracts or drunken musicians. What would life be like to own an inn like Nikki and Nate? Certainly a lot simpler. A long sigh escaped. Who knew what she'd face back in the land of fame and opportunity. With no word about the movie, Ron's last call wasn't encouraging. Could she salvage her career?

"I thought I was the only one who liked to brood," said a deep voice near her ear, snapping her back to the present.

The log shifted under his weight.

"Did someone tell you I used to call you that in college?" Red heat rose to her face, and not just from the sunburn.

He grunted. "You weren't the only one. Danny always said he'd been born the happy twin…" His voice trailed off, like he was remembering. He was quiet as he looked over at the lake.

"So, I hear you're famous?" His question broke the moment.

It was her turn to grunt. Famous for how long was the question. "Not really. I record and perform—mostly jazz venues. It's a living." She shrugged.

He bumped her shoulder in a playful way that had her heart flipping. He'd snapped out of brood mode again. "You're being modest. Gabe said you've won awards."

She rolled her eyes. "You and Gabe did a lot of talking, huh?"

He cleared his throat. "A bit. What, no boyfriend in the jazz world?" he asked, sounding uncertain and perhaps fishing for information.

"There's no one special." She tried to keep the answer casual and evasive. Was he interested or merely making conversation? Maybe that kiss meant more than she'd thought, and she'd thought a whole lot about it last night in bed. She sucked at deciphering guy signals. "What about you?"

"I wouldn't have kissed you if I had someone else," he stated, his brow furrowed.

Well, that answers that. "Why…" She paused. "I mean, why don't you, have someone?"

His blue eyes grew intense. "No offense, Tara, but I've been shot, watched people get shot, and ran through machine gun fire to drag out a fellow Marine. Those events change a person, big-time. And it's kinda hard to relate to any woman, or have any kind of relationship on a normal playing field after that."

Tara sucked in a ragged breath. Events in her life had changed her, shaped her, too. Motivation drove her. But was this why she avoided love like the plague? To avoid relating on a normal playing field, merely existing on the surface emotions fame brought? Only now her reasons for avoiding love seemed so plastic compared to his.

"When I stood on that tarmac and watched as Danny's coffin came off the plane, I thought, why in the hell wasn't it me? Not much to offer someone else when you feel that way about yourself, I suspect." He swallowed so hard that his Adam's apple rose.

Tara blew out a blustery breath and watched as his hands curled into fists. Her heart wept for him. This was real emotion. This was what she wrote and sang about, right here in front of her eyes. This was what her fans loved, why she did what she did—not necessarily for the fame it brought.

Todd coughed roughly and swiped at his eyes with his rag—the one with the leaves and twigs hanging off the end that he'd offered her earlier. The one she'd grimaced at and he'd laughed at her squeamishness. He didn't seem to notice, though. He was so at ease with nature. It calmed him, made him more personable. Just the way he interacted and joked with the group proved that. Nature somehow put him at peace.

Like music did for her. When she sat at the piano, all her troubles faded away.

He swiped at his face again and left behind a smudge on the side of his chiseled features. The group started to fuss around them, and there were grumblings of someone being hungry, but she ignored it.

She wanted to be the one to wipe away Todd's pain,

not the filthy rag. Whoa, where had that come from?

With purpose, Tara pulled the canteen strap over her head and unscrewed the cap. Cool water ran over her fingers and dripped onto her bare legs. She reached over and touched his cheek, lightly rubbing away the grime and hopefully some of his grief. His breath caught, then the hard set of his jaw relaxed and he closed his eyes to her touch.

"I'm really glad it wasn't you," she whispered.

His eyes registered surprise at first then his face took on that determined look; only a hint of vulnerability was left behind.

"You might be the minority. Danny being the happy twin, remember?"

"You couldn't have known what would happen or stopped that bitch from hurting Danny. It wasn't your fault." As she relayed the words, she tried not to think about what might happen to Janey, too, if this thing with Ben imploded.

"I should have protected him. If I'd never introduced them…" He shrugged. "Right after the stuff went down I made the vow to never waste another day doing something I didn't love. And doing it my way. Danny didn't get that chance, but I sure as shit can for him." He patted her knee as if to say "conversation over." She blinked at the sudden shift in his manner as he whistled for the group, then walked away.

But Todd's words hit home.

Had her professional life come at the sacrifice of her personal one?

Here she was hiding out in Maine until the bullshit of the world she wanted to be part of cleared? She rose from the log and a jagged rock punched at the sole of her sneaker. She kicked at it hard and it flew into the brush. She felt like a coward. Like she'd let Janey down by not getting on Ben to commit and do the right thing. By keeping quiet so her career might be saved.

Damn. This trip was more than she'd bargained for.

The guests thanked him and filed back to the inn and Todd walked behind Tara, trying not to breathe in her incredible scent. The more time he spent with her the more he wanted to, which surprised the hell out of him. Once again it'd been so easy to open up with her. What was it about her? Even with the bug spray, the hint of berries lingered in her hair. "You have some time? I want to show you something."

"Sure." She smiled slightly, but seemed troubled. Hell, he hoped his newly found flapping gums hadn't scared her.

He led her around the back of the inn along the path of concrete and limestone blocks to his two-story log structure. A short bark was followed by a soft whine and scratching on his front door.

"Is this your place?" she asked, her brows lowered in confusion.

He hopped up the two wide steps and nodded. "I plan to buy it once I finish the renovation." No woman—other than Nikki when she helped him move in—had ever come here. Felt a little awkward, but he didn't want his time with Tara to end yet.

As he unlocked the door, his houseguest charged out, yapping excitedly. Tara laughed and held out her hand as the dog ran back and forth between them.

"Lolita, settle down," he commanded, petting the dog behind the ears.

Her eyes widened. "Lolita? Interesting choice of names."

He grinned over his shoulder and motioned for her to enter into the open-layout living room. "Danny liked the book in college. It was all I could do to get through the CliffsNotes."

Her face had lit up and the sunburn she'd gotten on her nose made it shiny. "Big, strong Marine…fluffy poodle? What's wrong with this picture?"

"Well, she belonged to Danny, and Marissa wanted to send her to the pound. I had no choice but to take her in." He shrugged to make his words seems casual, but he'd grown to love the dog.

A flash of anger shone in Tara's eyes. "Again, I state, that woman is a bitch." Tara bent down and hugged Lolita, then gave her a kiss on the nose. "Oh my. Aren't you a doll."

When she got steamed she became sexier, if that were possible. *Settle down.* He cleared his throat and brought his thoughts and body under control. "You thirsty?" At her nod, he headed to the kitchen to cool off—in more ways than one.

When he came back, he found her admiring the floor-to-ceiling windows, which overlooked the endless woods. Tara touched every surface of the oak walls, the ledge where he kept photos of Danny, his folks, and his Corps buddies.

"You didn't tell me you have a piano." Tara motioned to the black baby grand.

"It was here when I moved in. Can't vouch for how it sounds, but I like the way it looks."

"Do you mind?" She pointed to the piano bench.

"Be my guest." He placed her water bottle on the top of the piano then sank onto his one indulgence—a large sectional, which practically wrapped around the entire room. The soft brown leather helped keep him cool in the summer heat.

His chest hitched at the first stirrings of the music. The slow melody was a mixture of sultry lows and sexy high notes. *Jeez.* He swallowed hard. Tara's face showed pure delight. She'd closed her eyes and let her fingers flow.

He wished it were his body she caressed and not the ivory keys.

He finally found his voice once the song faded to its end. "You're amazing. What was that?"

She rose and smiled shyly before sitting next to him, trying to smooth the wisps of hair sticking out all over her head. "'From This Day Forward.' It's the track I won the Grammy for."

"I can see why." He placed his arm behind her on the soft ledge of the couch and she moved an inch closer. "So what do famous musicians do for fun besides reciting every US president when a snake slithers by." He teased.

"Very funny." She laughed. "Sometimes when I get spooked, I do the president thing…"

He had to give her credit—even though she was clearly uncomfortable in the woods, she'd done her best trying to keep up with the rest of the group. "I'm just teasing. But seriously, do you have lots of famous friends?"

Her eyes darted away. "Famous friends? I have a few…unfortunately," she muttered. "I've been on tour for a while. But this weekend has been great."

His fingers dipped to her shoulder where soft skin covered the slender bone. "I'm going to go out on a limb here. I think you're great, Tara. I can't figure out why we never got to know each other better in college."

"I've got my own limb, okay?" She bit her lip again, all shy. "I had a *thing* for you in college," she confessed, rolling her eyes.

He stopped himself from grinning like a fool. "A thing? Umm…I'm not sure what that is."

She playfully punched his bicep and crossed her arms. "Don't make me say it."

He reached for her hand and caressed her palm. "I think I get it. Here's another limb. You're the most genuine person I've met in a hell of a long time. I don't know…maybe I'm jaded by all that shit with Danny and Marissa being a liar."

She tightened her lips and stared at her lap. "Todd, there's something I need to tell—"

Oh crap, had he said something wrong? His cell phone vibrating on the table broke the moment before he could find out. He leaned up and clicked it on. "Yeah," he answered. "Thanks, Nate." He hung up. She watched him curiously. "The supplies I need arrived. I have to get to the gazebo so it's finished for tomorrow's ceremony. What were you saying?"

"Um…nothing." She shook her head.

"I'll walk you to the lobby. But not before I do this." He pulled her to him and kissed her, long and slow.

♥♥♥

Tara almost made it to her room to change out of her crusty shorts and tank, but one last check of the piano in the ballroom had turned into a great moment with Nikki. What a wonderful songwriter Tara had discovered in the quiet innkeeper. Nikki was a real talent. Might be an idea to collaborate in the future, when Tara got her career back on track.

Leaving Todd was going to be hard, but at least they had the next day together. Her heart flipped thinking about his cozy cabin and their kissing…*phew*. A cold shower might be in order, too.

Tara pressed the button for the lobby elevator and waited. The more she got to know Todd, the more she liked him. It wasn't his amazing body, or his ability to kiss her into forgetting her name. No, he was genuine, too. Apprehension nagged at the back of her throat. The press painted her out to be someone she wasn't. Right after the rehearsal tonight, she'd tell Todd everything about the gossip.

Guess she could sort of understand the love Ben and Janey had found. But in this short a time, was it possible to have such a connection and longing for Todd?

Gabe and Viv stepped out of the elevator with an older couple. "Aunt Agnes and Uncle Albert," Gabe gestured, "this is our friend from college, Tara Graham. She's a famous musician."

Tara smiled at the pair.

The old man gaped at Tara's shorts, then up at her chest. He grunted when his wife's elbow connected with his ribs and Tara bit back a laugh.

The woman homed in on Tara's face and she pursed her lips. Wasn't she the creepy staring woman from yesterday?

"Now I remember, Albert." Agnes snapped her fingers, startling the man into dropping the muffin balanced on top of his takeaway coffee cup.

"She's that hussy on the cover of *Gossip Central* magazine."

Viv gasped. "Aunt Agnes! That's awful to say."

"No, no." Agnes wagged a hand practically under Tara's nose. "It's right here." Out of her quilted tote bag she pulled the latest edition—and that unflattering picture. Even though Tara had stared at it twelve million times on the net, the grainy photo still made her cringe. Guess she was indeed front-page news. "Just look at her…"

Shit. "I can explain—"

"That poor wife of his," the old woman mewed, completely cutting off Tara's defense. "It's terrible. Albert, you know that talented Amanda Cleary? This one here," she pointed at Tara with a sneer," is doing the horizontal mambo with her husband, Ben Pratt." The old woman's voice echoed through the lobby like a high-pitched drill.

Then the hairs on Tara's arms stood and her midsection started tingling. The feeling meant one thing... *No. No. No.* This could not be happening.

"And I saw her making moves on Morgan Stuart," Aunt Agnes bellowed. "Next, she'll be after my dear boy Todd. Really, Gabe, what kind of friends do you have? Or are they Genevieve's? I should have known." She harrumphed.

Heavy boot steps that had been crossing the floor stopped midstride and then silence. She didn't need to look up to see who it was.

If earthquakes occurred in Maine, now would be a good time for one to happen.

Against her better sense, she glanced at Todd.

His eyes were positively glacial.

With one false accusation his face said it all. In her gut she knew what he thought—she was a lying, cheating bitch, just like Marissa.

With tensed shoulders and without a sound, Todd strode out the door, taking a piece of her heart with him.

She turned to Viv. "I should have told him," she whispered. "It's not true." Viv's eyes widened with understanding at the anguish Tara knew had invaded her expression.

With a soft cry, Tara fled the lobby and bounded up the stairs as the tears leaked.

There is something to be said for manual labor kicking the shit out of being hurt on the inside. He'd attacked the rest of the gazebo repairs and set up for the wedding in record time. Groaning, he folded his sore self onto the couch.

Lolita jumped up and placed her fluffy head on his chest. "You're the only girl I can trust." Lolita whined and licked his face.

Tara Graham, with her innocent eyes and sweet-tasting mouth, turned out to be too good to be true. Was he just a distraction from her movie-star boyfriend? When it came to women, his judgment sucked.

Let's face it: she came from a different world. And two days of connecting and a few—okay, more than a few—hot kisses wouldn't change that reality. Was her sympathy about Danny even real? *Aw, hell.* He was as stupid as his twin to get sucked in by a beautiful face and smoking body.

This was why love, or lust, or whatever the seed of feeling in his chest for Tara was, didn't work, and never would.

A knock sounded and he considered not answering it. Lolita jumped down and barked, as if to say "answer the door, shithead."

"Fine," he muttered at the dog and opened the door.

Tara's eyes were red and puffy and he hardened himself against pulling her into his arms. Crying females made him feel like a heel. She was probably upset she'd gotten caught. Marissa had pulled the same shit on Danny.

"Can I come in?" She bit her bottom lip. He hated remembering the taste of her lips, so he forced himself to concentrate on a chipped spot on the doorjamb next to her face that needed paint.

"For what?" He kept his voice flat.

Her chin dropped a notch. "I'll just stay outside then," she said while ringing her hands. "Todd, what you heard Agnes say…it's not…"

"Not true?"

"Let me explain—"

"You know, Tara, it's okay. I get it." He shrugged one shoulder and crossed his arms. "You're on vacation, having fun, big music star, guy from college. I got to kiss a famous person. So yeah, I had fun, too."

Lolita scooted past and rubbed against Tara's legs. Tara looked at the dog with a confused hint of a smile and scratched behind her ears as Lolita peered back at him.

Great. Outnumbered.

Then the same fire he'd seen in Tara when she called Marissa a bitch reappeared. "Fun? Is that all this is between us? Wow." She laughed cynically. "I truly suck at guy signals."

Tara stepped in closer and he backed up an inch but she kept coming. Color rose to her cheeks. "You know," she sputtered and poked him in the middle of his chest, "you're not the only one who gets to protect their family. We may not know each other well, and it's useless apparently," she said sardonically, as if it were his fault she'd lied, "to try and convince you that some rag magazine just might be wrong…but you do not own the rights to the big sacrificial gestures."

Sure, blame the guy. Women were experts at that deflecting thing. No way was he buying it.

Then she took a deep breath and closed her eyes briefly before she squared her shoulders. "And for the record, it was more than just fun for me."

She turned on her heel and marched away. He watched her sexy saunter and something nagged at his slowly deflating anger. *Goddamn it*, should he believe her?

♥♥♥

Tara somehow made it through the wedding. The ceremony in the gazebo was perfect, and she gladly did a favor for Nate by playing Nikki's song.

Viv's face was radiant despite the worried glances she sent Tara's way. She felt bad about raining on Viv's parade, so she tried to crack a smile.

Tara did her best to sing the wedding song, John Legend's "All of Me" without breaking down into tears.

She had no movie, no gigs when she got home, and no man, either. Going from being on top of the world to feeling like a complete failure truly sucked.

Going a round with Bullwinkle had been the least of her problems in Maine.

She'd head home to Fat Lorenzo and start over. Forget about Todd and how he made her want to open up. Forget about how he'd made her want to face her feelings—if there were any for him she'd be willing to face, let alone comprehend. The bad publicity would die down, as it always did, and the next scandal would take front page.

Todd sat at the end of the bar with his arms crossed and a perpetual frown, which made a crevice in his perfect features.

Why should she care if he believed her or not?

If the weekend had taught her anything—besides what the ass end of a moose looked like—it was that her music was most important. Keeping with her roots, where she felt at home, mattered most. Not making movies, or being accepted in Hollywood, or avoiding front-page gossip.

A hush came upon the room. Tara turned to the flashes of cell phone cameras clicking away like mad.

"Is that Ben Pratt?" one of the groomsmen asked.

"What…uh…" Tara's mouth dropped open, then she made the mistake of looking straight at Todd. His face turned stony before he stormed out of the room.

Tara picked up her long gown so she didn't fall on her face. Best not grace another front page when the wedding guests loaded it onto social media.

Home wrecker takes a tumble. Karma?

"Why are you here, and where the hell have you been?" she whispered through gritted teeth as Ben made his way to her side.

Ben's anxious look when he spotted her turned to a wide smile and he stepped to the side. Janey came into view.

"Janey? Wha… I don't understand."

Her sister hugged her and then gave her the once-over. "You look like shit."

"I'm glad you said it." Ben laughed and put his arm around Jane's shoulder.

"Who's the guy who stormed out after he gave you the stink eye?" Jane always knew when something wasn't quite right—she had a knack for it.

A fat tear fell from Tara's eye before she had the time to process the surge of emotion rising up to her throat. "It's a long story."

"We only have a day so make it quick. Our honeymoon awaits." Ben beamed at Jane, who blushed.

Honeymoon? "What about Amanda?"

Ben smiled politely to the gathering crowd and found a corner of the room for them to talk. "We got a quickie divorce in Mexico," he explained in a low tone. "Besides, she's been having an affair with her publicist for the past year."

Her *publicist?* "Wow." That was the last thing Tara would have suspected. "But wait, you sounded so distraught," she said to her sister.

Jane crinkled her nose and bit her lip, guilty. "I didn't want you to worry. Besides, we eloped."

"And you're back on the movie," Ben informed her. "They've agreed to postpone shooting for a few weeks." Ben leaned down to place a kiss on Jane's brow.

They positively oozed love for one another.

"Thanks for taking the heat. I owe you." Jane hugged her again and laughed as the crowd of people who wanted Ben's autograph approached.

Talk about crashing a wedding, but Viv and Gabe didn't seem to mind, for they were first on line with beaming smiles.

Guess things worked out everywhere—Janey and Ben, Viv and Gabe, and the movie, of course. So why wasn't she happier? The answer had stormed out of the room…that's why.

"Flight 214 to LaGuardia Airport has been delayed due to rain in New York."

A few more hours in Maine, then she'd finally be done with nature and moose and…heartache.

Ben and Jane had dropped her off and were leaving on a later flight to Hawaii for their honeymoon. She and her Louis Vuittons were heading home to Fat Lorenzo. Although saying good-bye to Viv and Gabe had been sad, she'd promised to stay in touch this time.

Tara bent over her carry-on for her MP3 player, but the earbuds were a tangled mess among the stuff thrown in her bag last night…amidst the tears and champagne.

Leave it to Ben to ply her with alcohol and make her spill about Todd.

At least *they* were happier than two people could

possibly be. Janey with her science mind, and Ben, the creative one. Their kids would be a cross between Albert Einstein and Laurence Olivier.

As for her life? No love to be found. Not even a good, healthy dose of lust.

Career, then family, remember? Well, career, then who knew?

After the movie shoot, she'd focus on writing another song. Maybe she'd call this one "What Could've Been."

Tara straightened, looked to her left, and blinked. There was a pair of hiking boots on the next chair. *No, it couldn't be…* A familiar tingle started in her middle.

Day-old scruff covered his perfect face and his clothes were rumpled. Her mouth dropped open. "What happened to your cheek?"

Todd looked down in embarrassment and scratched the top of his head. "Someone decided I had the wrong opinion of you."

The baseball-sized bruise held hues of yellow and black against his tan. She shook her head in disgust. "Ben's an idiot." Todd had a few inches and at least fifty pounds on him. Her eyes narrowed. "Did you hurt him?"

"It wasn't Ben. Your sister has a mean southpaw."

She blinked. "Janey? When…wow." Who knew Janey was such a tough girl. Tara stifled a chuckle at the gloom on his face.

A flush crept across the non-bruised cheek. "This morning, and I deserved it. Me and my flapping gums due to a night with the bottle of Jack."

Could he be…apologizing? Tara tamped down any hope. "They didn't say anything." And they were both in big trouble.

Todd kneeled down in front of her and her breath caught. "I asked them not to. Tara…aw, hell…I suck at this stuff." He held her gaze and pushed the wayward piece of hair behind her ear.

She could seriously get used to that gesture.

"It's time I stop seeing the Marissa in everyone, especially when the most amazing person who has happened to me—*ever*—is nothing like her."

Her heart pounded but she wasn't going to let him off so easy. "And a bruise on the cheek convinced you?" She licked her lips with cautious hope.

Todd shook his head. "Nah. I realized you were something special the first minute after you went a round with Bullwinkle and came out making a joke. And when you got angry for Danny. And when I kissed you and you lit me up inside."

"Oh," she said, all breathy. *Girlie parts—singing a chorus.*

Todd picked up the boots and put them on her lap.

The tan suede was soft under her fingers. "Nice boots."

"They're for hiking," he said with a smirk. "Good for traction and long, slow walks in the woods."

She swallowed hard, finding it hard to stop the flutters in her body. "You plan on hiking a lot?"

"Not alone, I hope." Myriad emotions crossed his face, then a slow burn of awareness started from his lopsided smirk, straight to his eyes, and they positively smoldered.

"I'm not exactly the nature type, as you know. I might get lost." She tried to sound innocent.

He stood and took her with him. The boots clunked to the floor, but she didn't care. She tipped her head back.

"I won't let you get lost." He pulled her flush against the hard planes of his body and she sucked in a ragged breath. "I've never been to New York City before. Maybe you can show me around your neck of the woods."

Tara wound her arms around his neck and nuzzled his scruff as he let out a sexy growl. The sound sent tingles to her toes. "Not yet. I've got two weeks before I have to be in Toronto."

Todd tilted his head and captured her lips.

Maybe she could have love and a career, after all. And maybe her next song would be "What's to Come."

About…

Nicole S. Patrick has always loved to read, and in her teenage years, she "borrowed" her mom's books to sneak away and become lost in the world of romance. After more than ten years in the corporate world of tech recruiting and HR management, she decided to stay home and raise children. But with so many romantic stories and characters floating around in her head, when the kids napped, she was compelled to put those words on a page and pursue this crazy dream of becoming published. Nicole writes romantic suspense and her heroes are those alpha males in uniform. She lives in New Jersey with her real-life hero, her husband, and her two sons.

For more information about Nicole, please visit her website at www.nicolespatrick.com.

To Love
and Honor

Julie Rowe

♥♥♥

College sweethearts, Drew and Davina thought they'd be together forever, but after Davina catches Drew in a shower with a naked girl, she runs as far and as fast as she can. Away from him. Angry with her for not trusting him, Drew tries to date other girls, but realizes too late that Davina is it for him. She's long gone.

When a friend's wedding gives Drew the chance to apologize and make things right, he shows up at her door with his hat in his hand. Davina opens her hotel room door expecting to see her college roommate on the eve of her wedding, not Drew babbling about a misunderstanding and starting over. She finally gives him the response he deserves for breaking her heart, a bloody nose.

Drew's not giving up. He intends to show her he's her man, no matter how long it takes or how long he has to grovel. Davina is worth it.

♥♥♥

Dedicated to ~

My daughter Megan, whose bravery and perseverance humbles me every day. I love you.

To Love and Honor
by Julie Rowe

Moose Creek, Maine, hadn't changed a bit.

Davina Hobbs drove through the small town and noted the same businesses lining the main street as six years ago. The drug and grocery store, drive-in diner and barber shop.

The only thing that was different was the name of the county sheriff, Drew Cavendish.

Which was why she drove through town making sure to keep under the speed limit. Getting pulled over by Sheriff Cavendish was not an experience she wanted on this little pleasure trip.

She'd been to Moose Creek only once with her then boyfriend, the same Drew Cavendish. She'd been so in love with him, so certain they would make it.

Until the day she caught him with a naked girl in his shower.

It still hurt to think about it. The shame and

embarrassment at discovering he was just like all his football-playing friends who went from girl to girl to girl. Yet he'd begged her to listen to him, to take him back. After a week, she'd finally relented and went to see him, only to find him kissing yet *another* girl.

That was it. She was *done*.

She'd never spoken to him again.

Now she was driving through his town, on the way to a wedding where she would most likely have to look at him with whoever he was dating.

She made a silent vow to be the most law-abiding citizen Moose Creek had ever had.

If only her college roommate, Viv, and her fiancé, Gabe, had chosen a city venue for their wedding. Davina would have felt more comfortable with more escape routes available. The single road leading up to the inn hosting the wedding didn't allow speeds of more than thirty miles per hour. Hard to beat a hasty retreat when you had to dodge potholes.

Fifteen minutes later, The Loon Lake Inn appeared. The parking lot was already half-full with cars and trucks bearing license plates from several states.

No police vehicle in sight.

Davina blew out a breath she hadn't realized she was holding.

She went inside, registered at the desk, and made small talk with an elderly couple who were in the lobby. Agnes and Albert were Gabe's great-aunt and great-uncle and seemed excited about the wedding. When Davina told them she was Viv's college roommate—yes, the one that went on to be a doctor—they shook her hand repeatedly. Viv had talked about her more than once, said she was an important doctor in the city. Davina tried to explain that chief coroner wasn't all that big a deal—she dealt with dead bodies more than live ones—but they refused to believe her. It was…cute and sort of fun.

By the time she got to her room, she was smiling.

How long had it been since she felt anything but stress and loneliness? Months?

She really needed to get out more.

She settled for a hot shower and a comfortable summer dress to wear to meet up with Viv and Gabe.

A knock on her door had her smiling again. Viv was early.

Davina opened the door, preparing to give her friend a long hug, but it wasn't Viv in the doorway.

It was Drew.

An older Drew than the man she remembered.

This one was wearing a sheriff's uniform and had his hat in his hands. The broad shoulders, long eyelashes, and boyish smile were all the same, though. He looked in as good a shape as he'd been in college.

The impact of seeing him in her doorway, only a couple of feet away, was a blow to her chest. She'd thought the wound long healed, so why did it hurt so much to breathe?

"Hey, Davina," he said, that smile drawing a couple more wrinkles at the corners of his eyes. "I was hoping we could chat."

Chat? He wanted to *chat*?

The last time she'd talked to him—six years, one month, three weeks, and two days ago—he'd been in the arms of a very naked, very wet woman as they'd exited a shower.

She'd waited five entire seconds for him to begin to explain. Five seconds in which she endured the smirk of his naked playmate while he stared at her blankly then said, "Honey, you have no idea how glad I am to see you." No remorse in his expression. No regret.

That one phrase damn near killed her. A spear to her

heart. There were so many less painful ways to break up with a girlfriend than having her discover you with another woman *in flagrante delicto*.

Six years ago, she'd been thrown into a pit of despair.

But she wasn't that shy, too-smart-for-her-own-good, naive girl anymore.

Today, the smile on his face pissed her off and lit an unholy fire in her gut.

Davina pulled her arm back and punched him as hard as she could in the nose.

He stumbled back, his hands going to his face. "What the…" He pulled his hands away. A small trickle of blood rolled down to drip off his lip. He wiped at it, stared at the red then looked at her with wide, shocked eyes.

"Chat?" she demanded. "You want to *chat*? How about we talk about what a two-timing asshole you are? Or maybe we could discuss your lousy way of dumping your girlfriend? Huh?"

"You do realize you just assaulted a sheriff?" he asked, his voice incredulous.

She crossed her arms over her chest. "You're lucky I didn't kick you in the nuts."

"I never cheated on you," he said, a little muffled by the sleeve he was using to stop the bleeding. "I didn't know who that girl was."

"Well, your hand on her ass told a different story."

"She walked into the shower and grabbed me. I couldn't get her out of there without putting my hands someplace."

"So you chose the crack of her butt?"

"My hand slipped!"

"Really?" she said, enough sarcasm dripping off her words to burn a whole through metal. "So did mine."

She slammed the door, engaged the lock, and glared at it. If he knocked again, she wasn't going to be so nice.

What the hell just happened?

Drew stared at the closed door like it shielded the secrets of the universe. All he'd wanted was to talk, maybe offer an apology for what happened six years ago and get one in return for Davina not believing him.

Hoping for a fresh start was probably a little more than was realistic, but a punch in the face hadn't been on his radar at all.

Drew pulled his hand away from his nose and looked down at himself. Jeez, he was covered in blood and it was still dripping off his face.

With one last look at Davina's hotel room door, he headed toward the lobby and the nearest exit. Three steps into the lobby, he knew he'd made a mistake. It was full of incoming wedding guests, including an elderly couple related to the groom.

Agnes and Albert looked up from their wedding invitation as he walked in.

"Good heavens, Sheriff, sit down before you fall down," Agnes said.

"Agnes, he can look after himself," Albert told her. He took a second look at Drew and grunted. "Or maybe not."

"He's bleeding," she yelled, one decibel below a scream. Agnes pinned her glare on him and said, "Sit."

Drew sat.

Noelle, who was manning the check-in desk, rushed over with a box of tissues and handed him a couple.

Agnes put her hands on her hips and shook her head. "You look like you've bled enough for two men."

She turned her glare on the clerk. "What room is that nice lady doctor in?" She snapped her fingers a couple of times. "Davina. Please ask her to come take a look at Sheriff Cavendish's nose."

Drew had to hide his smile behind his shirtsleeve. "Thanks, Agnes." He was happy to milk her interference for all it was worth. "It's still bleeding."

"Did you arrest the idiot who hit you?" Albert asked, looking around. "Did you call for backup?"

Drew winced. There were way too many police and crime dramas on TV these days. "Um, no. I tripped and whacked my face on a doorknob."

Agnes stopped her fussing and Albert stopped looking for someone large enough to have beat Drew up to stare at him with their jaws open for two long seconds.

"A doorknob?" Agnes's voice was high with disbelief.

A commotion near the entrance to the inn caught his attention. A flurry of people were arriving with luggage. Albert backed out of the way, leaving the newcomers with a clear view of Drew in his blood-splattered shirt.

Two women mixed in with the crowd gasped his name and came rushing over. Leanne Mosby and Tammy Strickland were far more dangerous than any small-time crook. They were both divorcees looking to find a new man to call their own. They'd set their sights on him last year and had managed to become quite a nuisance to him and his whole office. He'd move, but this was his hometown.

Did the two of them have a bet going on as to who would land him?

Leanne was a blonde with manicured fingernails that were long enough that he wondered how she did anything at all without them getting in the way.

Tammy was a brunette who was too skinny for the

massive rack she displayed in low-cut, tight shirts that left nothing to the imagination.

Leanne hip-checked Agnes out of the way with a skill that would have made any NHL hockey player proud. She put her hand, and her dazzling sharp nails, on his neck. Tammy scooted around behind him, grabbed his arm, and turned him toward her.

Leanne tightened her grip on his neck while Tammy yanked harder on his arm, both complaining to the other that they were helping him.

At this rate, they were going to cause more damage than the punch to his face.

"This is the medical emergency?" an irate female voice asked.

Davina. Thank God.

"He looks like he's got all the helping hands any man could want and then some," Davina drawled.

Leanne smiled—at least he thought it was supposed to be a smile—and said in a throaty voice, "It's just a little nosebleed. No need for everyone to panic. I'll take the sheriff home and wash his shirt for him."

"My house is closer," Tammy said. "And I have a brand-new washing machine that takes half the time yours does. He should come with me."

Davina started laughing loud enough to draw everyone's attention. And kept on laughing until she was bent over and gasping for air.

Davina wouldn't have believed this situation was happening if she hadn't watched it unfold. Drew Cavendish was about to get ripped in half by two desperate and dateless housewives.

The blonde sneered at her. "Laughing at an injured

man is despicable."

"I don't know who you are," the brunette said with her nose in the air, "but this isn't funny. Can't you see he's hurt?"

"With nosebleeds," Davina told them, "it almost always looks worse than it is. Besides, I'm the one who hur—"

"Is the doctor," Drew interrupted.

"You two heifers get your hands off the sheriff," Agnes ordered, her eyes flashing with anger. "Neither one of you has the smarts God gave a squirrel."

The two women sputtered, but didn't let go of Drew.

"How dare y—"

"What a rude thing to sa—"

"You're choking him," Davina interrupted, looking at the blonde's hand on his neck. "You might want to let him go before you murder your precious sheriff."

Drew's face had turned a dark red.

Both women released him and stepped back with gasps of worry and incoherent apologies.

Drew coughed and sucked in air with more effort than was strictly necessary.

Drama king.

Agnes took over, flapping her hands at the two women. "Go on now and let a professional deal with the situation. All you two are doing is causing a scene."

Davina had to work to keep the smirk off her face as she came around to look at Drew's nose. She pulled his wrist and bloody sleeve away from his face. Blood dripped slowly.

She grabbed a couple of tissues, put them in his left hand then picked up his right hand and brought it up to the bridge of his nose. "Pinch here. The bleeding should stop in a few minutes."

Drew mumbled something, but it came out garbled.

Before Davina could ask him to repeat it, Agnes clicked her tongue at him. "You sound like you have a mouth full of marbles, Sheriff. Best to stop talking until the worst is over."

Worst what? Two women were fighting over who was going to take him home. Most men would be happy in his situation.

"Poor man." Agnes shook her head. "You work too hard." She turned to Davina and said in a conspiratorial tone, "He doesn't get enough sleep having to deal with criminals and silly geese like those two who were yanking on him like a wishbone."

Drew sighed with exaggerated patience.

Davina bit her lips to prevent smiling. "Oh?"

"Nag him half to death, they do. I'll bet that's why he tripped, too tired to see where he was going."

She had to stifle a snort. Is that what he'd told people? "Perhaps if he just picked one, the rest would leave him alone. Or does he prefer to keep his options open?"

"Oh no, Sheriff Cavendish doesn't date."

That seemed unlikely. "Really? Why not?" She looked him over. It was impossible to miss his mouthwatering muscle tone. She shouldn't needle him, but she couldn't help observing in a fake concerned tone, "He seems handsome enough and has a good job."

"You'd think the world was his oyster," Agnes agreed, then leaned closer and said, "For a while there, the townsfolk wondered if he liked men more than women."

Drew choked and coughed until his breathing wasn't much more than wheezing.

Davina smacked him on the back with a couple of gratifying thumps.

"But finally," Agnes continued, "the sheriff told

everyone how he'd lost the love of his life to a misunderstanding. He's still pining for her." She shook her head. "Very sad."

"There's always two sides to every story," Davina replied, pulling some wet wipes from her first-aid kit and wiping the blood from Drew's face. "Maybe the woman in question discovered him cheating on her."

His brows came down in rebuke.

She frowned right back at him.

Agnes shook her head. "I can't believe that. I've seen the sheriff turn down every woman in town, including a recent wealthy widow and several attractive younger ladies who would make a good wife for a sheriff. Good girls who are smart, but also want to stay home and raise a family."

Anger overtook Davina as she finished cleaning Drew's face and nose. Too bad she didn't have some steel wool to scrape the blood off with. "He should have taken one of those fine young ladies up on their offer of a warm home with children. Not every woman can provide that. Take me, for example. As a doctor, I work a lot and I'm seldom at home."

"Your work is important." Agnes patted Davina on the arm. "I'm sure there's a man out there who appreciates that."

Davina gave Drew a significant look. She shouldn't have bothered. Drew wasn't interested in her.

"Thank you, but I'm comfortable with my life as it is." She looked Drew in the eyes and said with complete sincerity, "You really shouldn't wait too long to get married to one of those pretty, nice girls chasing you. You deserve a good life."

Drew's eyes widened.

Davina's stomach dropped like a stone. He was going to know she still…cared. What had she just said?

Drew watched the color drain from Davina's face and knew she was about to bolt. She'd done it before. He'd watched her run out of a room and he hadn't seen her again for six long years.

Not this time.

This time, she wasn't getting away that easily. She was going to have to convince him she didn't still have feelings for him, and from her last couple of sentences, he had doubts she could do that.

She cared. He might have to remind her how much, but she cared.

Before she could take off running, he wrapped his hand around one of her wrists. "Thank you for your concern." He wanted to sound serious, but his plugged nose made him sound like he had the world's worst cold.

She pulled at her arm and he let her go. Slowly.

Davina jerked her gaze away from his and smiled at Agnes and Albert, then began backing away. She glanced at him, but didn't stop moving. "If the bleeding doesn't stop in another fifteen minutes, let me know and I'll take another look." She turned and hurried away.

After she was out of sight, Agnes and Albert both looked at Drew. "You're an idiot if you let that woman get away from you again," Agnes said.

Surprise had him staring at the older couple. "How did you know?"

"We're old, not dumb," Albert explained. "You have no idea the chase this gal led me on before we got married."

Agnes gave her husband a saucy grin. "It was worth every second."

"That it was, my darlin'." Albert patted his wife on the butt. "The good ones always take work," he told Drew. "If she's the right one, she'll appreciate the effort."

"Grovel, you mean?"

"That's only part of it," Albert cautioned with a shake of a finger. "You've also got to show her how much you love her. It's the little things, son, that make the most difference."

"The little things aren't really all that little to a woman," Agnes added. "Every morning Albert brings me a cup of coffee before I get out of bed. He's been doing it every day since the day we got married."

"When our kids came along," Albert said with a faraway look on his face, "I started doing the dishes every evening after dinner to give Agnes a break. It turned out to have an unexpected consequence."

A blush brought a rosy glow to Agnes's face. "Ain't nothing sexier than a man doing dishes."

There was a mental image he didn't need in his head.

"I think I've got it." Drew got to his feet. "I have some plans to make."

Albert winked. "Go get her, Sheriff."

"I will." Drew strode over to the registration desk. First, he needed a room at the inn.

The ice had melted in Davina's Long Island Iced Tea. She took a sip and made a face at the watered-down flavor. She didn't know why she was still here, at the inn's bar surrounded by drunk women, watching those same women consume free drink after free drink.

"Okay, who died?" Viv asked her with narrowed eyes as she sat on the bar stool next to Davina. Viv's friend Margot sat on the stool on the other side. "You look so depressed you're bringing me down with you."

Davina sighed. "I ran into Drew today."

"Oh yeah, Aunt Agnes said you helped him with a bloody nose. That surprised me. I thought you said you wouldn't help him unless he was at death's door."

Davina sipped a little bit more of her watered-down drink. "Yeah, well, I'm the one who gave him the bloody nose."

Viv and Margot stared at her for a second, then burst out laughing.

"Really?" Viv asked.

Davina nodded. "I opened my hotel room door and there he was, asking if we could talk. I got so mad I punched him in the face."

Viv laughed hard enough that she fell off her bar stool. It took her a minute to get up off the floor and make it back to her seat, but once she did she ordered a round of shots. "This we have to celebrate. I'd have paid money to see it."

"He was surprised." She'd surprised herself, too.

"I'll bet."

The bartender placed the shots in front of them and Viv, Margot, and Davina tossed them back.

"You know, he really hasn't dated. He tried, but his heart was never in it." Viv looked at her with an arched eyebrow. "I wonder where it was?" Before Davina could come up with a response, Viv continued with a far easier question. "Then what happened?"

"He went out to the lobby where he ran into Gabe's great-aunt and great-uncle."

"Agnes and Albert?" Viv asked. "They're everywhere. The worst gossips in the family."

"She sent for me to take a look at his nose. When I got there, two women were arguing about who was going to take him home to clean him up and wash his clothes. Agnes didn't seem too thrilled about that idea and said a few choice words to them." Davina smiled at the memory of the expressions on the two women's faces. "Honestly, I couldn't stop myself from laughing."

"Agnes has a sharp tongue," Viv agreed. "I think that calls for another shot." She signaled for another round then said to Davina, "Not sure why she asked for you right off. She's a retired nurse."

"She is?" Agnes had looked completely clueless. "She didn't say anything or try to help Drew." Gossip? Ha. Instigator was more like it.

The bartender delivered the drinks and they tossed them back.

Viv carried on with her assessment of her soon-to-be great-aunt, "She likes to play matchmaker. Ten bucks says she saw an opportunity to put you and Drew together and took it."

"He told her about me?" It came out as a squeak, but she couldn't help it. She'd almost choked on her drink.

"Nope. Drew never told anyone who the long-lost love of his life is. Just that he lost her because he was stupid. Agnes is good at that shit."

Davina snorted. "At least he got the stupid part right."

Viv giggled. "That calls for another shot."

Davina lost count of the shots after four. There might have been two more after that, or maybe it was three. She didn't care. She was drunk and damned if it didn't feel good to not care about anything.

Drew could play with all the housewives he wanted. No skin off her nose.

Nose. Davina snorted at the thought. She'd punched his hard enough to make it bleed and she was proud of herself.

He'd had that coming for a long time.

"Okay," she said to Viv and abandoning her bar stool. "I'm going to bed, though after all these shots, I may be going to the bathroom first."

"Are you okay to get to your room?" Viv asked, blinking at her as if a few extra flaps of her eyelashes might clear up her vision.

Davina smiled brightly. "Yup." And trundled off.

She managed to get her hotel room door open after a few tries, but stopped after a step or two inside. Whose flowers were those?

She checked the door number. Yep, this was her room. She glanced at the huge bouquet of roses on the dresser. Where the hell had those come from?

She walked over unsteadily and managed to grab the card without knocking the whole thing over.

Thanks, Drew.

Thanks? For what? A nosebleed? What did he want next time, black eyes?

Next to the flowers was a box of fancy chocolates.

What the hell was wrong with him that he gave her flowers and chocolates after she assaulted him?

Idiot.

Davina grabbed the flowers and chocolates and weaved her way out her door and to the hotel room Drew had written on the card. She was not going to have these stupid things in her room where she could see them and eventually feel guilty enough to thank him for them.

Damn him. She already felt guilty.

She found his room and knocked hard on the door.

It opened to reveal a woman in purple lingerie. One of the two who had fought over Drew in the lobby. Tammy?

"Oh, it's you," the woman said, losing her simpering, seductive expression. "What do you want?"

"I'm surprised to see you. Didn't Agnes send you home?" Davina asked with smirk.

Tammy smiled in the fake plastic way of a used-car salesman. "Sheriff Cavendish invited me over."

Davina glanced over the bimbo's shoulder, but didn't see Drew anywhere.

Bullshit.

Then again…

"These must belong to you, then." Davina held out the box of chocolates. As soon as Tammy took them, Davina tossed the entire contents of the vase—flowers, water, and all—in the other woman's face. "And these. Enjoy."

Tammy screeched, but Davina turned and left before she laughed in the other woman's face. Besides, there was nothing for her in Drew's room except more disappointment and another woman waiting for him to return.

Where the hell was he, anyway?

Davina paused in the hallway, then decided on a slightly different direction. Back to the inn's bar.

It was busy with locals, wedding guests, and, yes, the groom's party with Drew in the middle of the pack, a beer bottle dangling from his fingers. How dare the rat look relaxed and happy?

She stomped over to him, shoving a couple of guys out of the way when they tried to offer her a drink. "There you are," she said.

He looked up and smiled like he really was happy to see her. "Hey, Davina, would you like to join us?"

Chat, join—he was all about the casual, the surface. She needed a man who could handle the dark parts of her, as well as the light. "Join you…you jerk. No, thanks."

His smile fizzled out and he frowned. "What did I do now?"

She thrust a finger under his nose and shook it at him. "How dare you give one woman flowers and candy, then invite a different woman for a private party in your hotel room? Have you no shame?"

His body jerked like she'd shocked him. "Say what?"

"You heard me, you two-timing jack…jack…o'-lantern."

"I think you mean jackass," Gabe corrected helpfully.

"Yeah." Davina pointed at Gabe. "That."

"Drew sent you flowers?" Gabe asked with great interest.

Drew covered his face with one hand. "Here we go."

"Yeah, but…" Davina wobbled for a moment before she smiled brightly and rediscovered her equilibrium. "I gave them to the woman in his room."

His hand dropped into his lap. "There's a woman in my room?"

"Yup. Tossed the flowers and water all over her face and fancy negligee." She snickered. "You'd better get back there before there's a noise complaint from your neighbors. She was screaming pretty loud when I left."

"I didn't invite anyone to my room," Drew protested.

"The card you left with the flowers sure seemed like an invite to me," Davina said.

Drew's mouth opened and closed a couple of times before he sputtered, "Yeah, but I didn't invite anyone else."

"How did she get into your room, then?"

"I don't know."

She rolled her eyes. "Again with the *oh, poor me, I don't know how that naked woman got into my room or shower*."

"That was six years ago." Drew threw his hands in the air. "And I didn't invite that one, either."

"You're such a creek." Davina had to blink to keep the world from spinning.

"I think you mean creep," Gabe offered in between chuckles.

"Yeah. Creep." The room really was going around fast. "I should have known better than to believe a hot guy like you was really interested in me for more than sex two or three times a day."

Gabe's mouth dropped open. "Two or three...*every* day?"

Davina sniffed. "It wasn't my fault I had so much studying to do. I was trying to get into medical school."

Gabe turned an envious expression on Drew. "Dude, teach me."

Drew groaned. "Someone fucking shoot me."

His words seemed to come from a long distance away. The light in the room dimmed, turning all the people in the bar into indistinct shadows and ghosts.

Gravity stopped working about the same time all the lights went out.

Drew managed to catch Davina before her head hit the side of the table.

Next to him, Gabe lost his battle with keeping his laughter in. "Wow, I have never seen her this drunk before."

"Me neither." He'd have to watch her closely to make sure she didn't throw up while she was still out.

Gabe punched him on the shoulder. "You dog. Every day? Holy shit, man, what the hell kind of pills were you popping back in college and why didn't you share?"

"I didn't need any damn pills. Davina is fucking gorgeous. I couldn't keep my hands off her." He still couldn't.

"So what's with the women getting into your room?"

"I don't know." He looked down into the face of the

woman he'd never been able to get out of his system or his heart. "But I'm going to find out." He stood and hoisted her over his shoulder. "Catch you later."

Gabe shook his head. "I can't wait to hear how this goes down. Talk to you tomorrow."

Drew got halfway back to his room before Davina woke up.

"Hey," she said in a slurred voice. "What's going on?"

Drew decided answering her would be more dangerous than keeping his mouth shut, at least until they got to his room.

"Drew, put me down."

He didn't answer, just hurried along a little faster.

"I'd know your ass anywhere."

Keeping his mouth closed wasn't helping. "Huh, we'll discuss that later, after we've had a little chat."

"Put me down, you Neanderthal."

He kept his tone even. "Nope, you're drunk."

It was a full two seconds before she said, "But I'm not driving. You can't arrest me for drunk walking."

"I'm not arresting you. I'm trying to figure out what the hell is going on, and until I do," he lowered his voice into what his deputies called his all-business tone, "you're not leaving my sight."

She was silent for all of two seconds. "I demand private time to pee."

God save him from drunk women. "You are going to hate yourself tomorrow morning."

"Ha, I already do." She sniffed again. Was she crying? Before he could ask, she ordered in an imperious tone, "Now put me down."

Since they'd arrived at his room, and the door was open, he did as he was told. Once Davina was on her feet he slowly let her shoulders go.

She stumbled into the room and almost tripped over the housekeeping lady who was picking up the last of the flowers on the carpet. The inn had hired a couple of temp workers from a couple towns over to help with all the extra people and events over the weekend.

"Well," Drew said, "at least you got the part about throwing the flowers on someone right."

"I didn't throw them on her," Davina said, pointing at the housekeeper.

"I'm sorry, sir," the lady said. "Your wife is in the shower."

"Wife?" Davina asked.

"Wife?" Drew repeated. "I'm not married."

"That's who she said she was," the housekeeper said, horrified. "Earlier when I let her in. She said she'd forgotten her room key."

Davina looked down her nose at him. "You have a big problem with women."

"Only one?"

She rolled her eyes. "I want to go back to my room."

Drew couldn't think of a better idea. "Let's go, twinkle toes."

"You can stay in your own room."

"No, thanks. It comes with an accessory I really don't want."

"Ha. Funny." She started off down the hall.

Drew had to keep her from falling on her face only twice.

When they reached her room, she tried unsuccessfully to get the key into the lock on the door several times before Drew took it from her and opened it.

"Thanks," she told him. "You can go now."

As if. "You don't look so good. I think I'll stay to make sure you're okay."

"I'm fine," she said, waving her hands at him. "All I

need to do is throw up a few times, and I'll be awesome."

"When are you planning on doing that?" She was almost green enough to pass for a frog.

"Is now too soon?" she asked, covering her mouth with one hand.

Drew grabbed her and rushed her into the bathroom just in time for her to puke in the toilet. He gave her a few minutes to retch without him hovering over her, then wet a washcloth with warm water and wiped her face with it. "Better?"

"Not really," she said as she laid her head on the side of the porcelain bowl. "Tired."

"You going to throw up some more?"

"No…" Her voice tapered off into a sigh.

Drew picked her up and laid her on the bed. He took off her shoes, her pants, and top and tucked her under the covers. He tried really hard not to look, but couldn't help notice that she'd only gotten more gorgeous since he'd last seen her. There was a maturity to her muscle tone that was sexy in a way that caught him by the testicles and didn't let go.

He made himself take a step back and put her room key in his pocket. He was going to figure out who had invited herself into his room and make sure they never did it again. Then he was going to come back.

He wasn't going to let Davina run away this time.

Davina was going to smash the telephone three inches from her head into tiny, tiny bits. The shrill scream amplified her headache into an earthquake. She reached out blindly, fumbling around until she found the receiver.

"Hello," she croaked.

"Dr. Hobbs, this is the front desk. We have a hotel

guest who's experiencing chest pain. He's refused to go to a hospital, but another guest has convinced him to let you look at him. Would you mind?"

Any other day she would have been happy to. Today, even her hair hurt. How much had she drank last night? "Where is he?"

"Here in the lobby."

"I'll be there in a few minutes." She hung up the phone, rolled over, and came face-to-face with Drew.

She sucked in a breath so fast it cut her throat to ribbons. "*Holy shit.*"

"Who was that?" he asked.

"What the hell are you doing in my bed?" Had she drank enough to invite him to her room? Wait, she was in her underwear and under the covers. He was fully clothed and appeared to have slept on top of the covers.

"You were pretty unstable on your feet last night, so I carried you back here. Unfortunately, that was when the alcohol caught up to you and you started throwing up. You passed out in the bathroom, so I cleaned you up a little and tucked you into bed."

"And you invited yourself, too?" It came out a screech.

"No, I was scared you might vomit while you were out cold, so I made the decision to stay. How's your hangover?" His tone was concerned, solicitous, even kind.

She narrowed her eyes. "I hate you."

"That bad, huh?"

"Get out of my room."

"I didn't invite Tammy to my room last night."

Memory flooded in—the flowers and chocolate she'd decided to return to him, only to find the stacked brunette waiting for Drew in a flimsy lace outfit that didn't cover anything.

"I threw the flowers on her." She laughed.

"Yeah." He smiled. "I wish I had been there to see it." He rolled off the bed and onto his feet. "If this keeps up I'm going to charge her with harassment."

Davina couldn't tell if he was joking or not. "Yeah, whatever. I've got to go. Someone might be having a heart attack in the lobby." She swung her feet to the floor and levered herself to her feet.

Drew's eyebrows rose even as his eyes traveled her body. "They call for an ambulance?"

"Hey, I'm up here," she said, pointing at her face.

He didn't look the least bit sorry as he met her gaze.

"No. Whoever it is, they're refusing to go."

He glanced at her breasts. "You going looking like that?"

God, he was such a guy. She shook her head and went into the bathroom. It didn't take long to use the toilet, brush her teeth, and stick her head in the sink to get her hair wet. When she came out Drew was gone.

About time. Waking up next to him had been a shock. For a moment she'd been taken back in time to those mornings when she woke next to him while they were dating. She'd kiss him awake and make long, slow love, the pleasure exquisite.

Loss twisted her stomach into an even tighter, painful knot.

Those days were over.

Davina got dressed, grabbed the first-aid kit she always traveled with, and made her way to the lobby.

Drew was already there, asking people to move back.

He looked up and saw her. "Please, folks, the doctor is here. Make a little more room for her to work."

The half dozen people stepped aside, giving her an unobstructed view of an older man sitting in an armchair.

His face was pale and coated in a sheen of sweat. His

lips were tinged with blue, almost as if he were wearing lipstick. His breathing sounded labored without a stethoscope and he rubbed his left arm like it hurt.

She approached him, and Drew got the crowd to move back another couple of feet. "Hello, I'm Dr. Hobbs. What's your name, sir?"

He huffed and puffed as he replied, "Richard Zimmerman."

"How long have you been experiencing pain and shortness of breath?"

"About twenty minutes."

She pulled out her stethoscope. "I'm going to listen to your chest, okay?"

"Okay, but I don't want to go to a hospital."

Drew shushed everyone without making any of their audience mad. Now that was talent.

Davina listened to the man's chest. His breathing was very tight and his heart rate was odd. The beat wasn't steady—there were missing beats, or they were cut short. "Richard, you're going to a hospital. I'm afraid you've got no choice. What you do get to choose is how you're going to go. Either you go in an ambulance or a body bag."

Richard's eyes widened. "It's that bad?"

She nodded. "Yes, it is. So which do you want?"

He closed his eyes. "Ambulance."

A few feet away, Drew ordered the ambulance with his cell phone. "ETA, ten minutes."

Davina spent the next few minutes asking Richard questions about his medical history, medications, and if he'd experienced these symptoms before.

When the paramedics arrived, she gave them a concise report and suggested treatment.

"Why can't you just order them to give the medication?" Drew asked as one of the paramedics called in to the hospital to get permission to administer the medication Davina suggested.

"I don't have ordering privileges at this hospital, and I'm from out of state." She put her stethoscope away. "It would be like you doing what a sheriff from another state told you to do."

"Huh, I never thought about it that way."

"Plus, I'm a coroner, not an ER doctor. They might have different medication regimens in practice here than I know about, or have kept up with."

"Why a coroner?" He scratched his head. "You're good with people. Why would you choose to work with the dead?"

"Because I'm too much of a people person."

He scratched his head. "Explain that to me."

"I struggle with maintaining an emotional distance between patients and myself. I have no problem with the dead. Someone has to speak for them, discover if foul play, neglect, or carelessness was involved in their death. I do that. But with living patients, I got too emotionally invested in all of them. It was tearing me apart even during my residency." She ground to a halt. Why had she told him all that? She cleared her throat and finished with, "My mentor suggested I try the morgue for a while and that's where I discovered my place. I like solving a puzzling death."

"Yeah, you always were a softy at heart," he muttered.

"Has your curiosity been satisfied?" she asked.

"I suppose."

"Good." She turned and walked back to her room.

He followed her. The man was worse than a puppy.

She stopped at the door before unlocking it. "What now?"

"We need to talk."

He'd always been persistent; the past few years had just put a shine on it. "Back to that, are we?"

"I'm not going to stop asking," he said, taking a half step closer, crowding her against the door.

Anger straightened her back and she unlocked the door. The room looked the same as when she left it. The bed in disarray, her clothes from the night before thrown on the desk chair.

She turned and put her hands on her hips. "Okay, now's your chance. Talk."

Drew ran a hand threw his hair and looked at the floor for a couple of seconds. Finally, he met her gaze with a rueful one of his own. "I'm sorry." He sighed. "I'm sorry for not making it clear six years ago that the girl in the shower wasn't there on my invitation. I'm sorry for not chasing after you to explain, even though I was buck naked. I'm sorry for being an idiot and kissing another girl to find out if what we had was as good, as special, as I thought."

Every word out of his mouth cut her heart to ribbons all over again. "You weren't sure what we had was special?" She'd known it from the moment they met.

"I admit I was stupid. I had all these friends telling me that one girl was as good as another, and I was so angry that you didn't trust me, I decided they were right."

Every word he said hit her like blows to the body, robbing her of breath, strength, and the ability to think.

"They said I didn't need you, I just needed a warm body, but I found out the hard way that they were wrong."

The knot in her stomach twisted tighter, the pain making her eyes water with tears she refused to shed while he was watching. "That's really dumb."

"Yeah, I knew it the second I kissed that other girl. There was nothing there. Nothing at all. When I kissed you, I stepped into paradise." He stared at her with eyes hot with need, his fists clenching and unclenching.

He wanted her.

Her own body responded to the need stamped on him, her heart rate and breathing increasing. "You should go now."

"We're not done." His voice was rough with desire.

"You're forgiven. There," she said, backing up a step. "You've apologized, I've forgiven you, we're done."

One corner of his mouth kicked up and he took a step toward her. "I don't want to go."

She retreated. "You should."

He followed her. "I want to kiss you again."

Her breathing stuttered. "That's not a good idea."

He tilted his head to one side. "Why not? Because you're afraid you'll like it?"

Her back hit the wall next to the bathroom. "Yes." Hell, she'd *love* it.

He put his hands on either side of her face and leaned down until his lips were only a couple of inches from her own. "I've been starving for a taste of your kiss for six years." His breath came in pants and his pupils were huge. "Please."

She opened her mouth to say no, but she hesitated, remembering the pleasure his kisses had given her.

Big mistake. His eyes flared and he covered her lips with his own.

She moaned into his mouth as his tongue tangled with hers. So good. Better, hotter than she remembered. Sensation and need arrowed through her body, making her ache for more than a kiss.

His shoulders were hard with muscle beneath her hands, his legs thicker and harder than before, and when he thrust one thigh between her legs, she found herself rocking against it.

He shifted, his hands on her waist to lift her up on that thigh, while he rubbed his erection against her lower belly.

Her breath caught. His cock was a long, luscious length that had filled her until she'd been afraid he wouldn't fit. The ache between her legs intensified until all she could think about was finding relief.

One of his big hands cupped her breast and she couldn't keep the moan from escaping her throat. His thumb found her nipple and teased it with little touches, as if he were asking permission.

She put her hand over his and pressed his palm against her flesh.

When she let go, he used his index finger and thumb to pinch and roll her nipple, sending a whip of pleasure so intense through her body that she jerked.

Her hands pulled at his shirt as she kissed him frantically, desperate to feel his skin against her own, his hands on her body, his cock inside her.

He pulled back and closed his eyes. "Davina?"

She didn't want questions—she wanted him. Now.

She put her hand on his erection and squeezed.

He lost it.

His hands yanked at her shirt and sent it flying as soon as it cleared her head. Her bra lasted even less time, but he stopped to stare at her breasts. They were fuller now than in college, overfilling his hands as he cupped them with a reverence that had her swallowing down a whimper.

He ducked his head and put his mouth on one nipple and she keened aloud how much she loved it. She wrapped one leg around his and tried to climb him, but he was too tall.

He picked her up and carried her to the bed, not letting her go or pausing in the exquisite attention he was giving to her breast.

Then he switched to the other breast and she couldn't stop the sounds emerging from her throat. Her hands tried to get his pants off, but she was unable to manage anything beyond hanging on to him as he brought her to the edge of orgasm with his mouth and hand on her nipples alone.

He finally moved from her breast to her neck, nipping and sucking his way up to her ear. His hands pulled her pants and panties off, his palms and fingers stroking her butt before dipping between her legs to tease the hypersensitive entrance to her body.

"Drew, please, I need…" She couldn't finish, couldn't get the words out through a throat that was already too tight.

"Are you sure, Dav? God, please be sure because I don't think I'll be able to stop once I get inside you." He rested his forehead against her own and growled, "It's been so fucking long."

"N…now, Drew. *Now.*"

He moved, shifted, the feel of denim replaced by hot skin, and then he was there, the head of his cock pushing inside of her.

She arched her back as he continued his slow penetration, wanting to take all of him.

His body shook as he finally seated himself inside her. "Holy shit." Then he moved and she stopped thinking altogether. There was only the slide of her skin against his, his cock stroking the ache inside her, tightening it into a ball of pleasure, while he muttered unintelligible words in her ear.

He changed his angle slightly and hit a spot inside her that detonated that tight ball of nirvana until it burned through her whole body, setting her on fire.

When she came back to herself, he'd stopped his

deep thrusts in favor of little flexes of his pelvis that served to tease all the nerve endings inside her. *How was he doing that?*

He hovered over her, nose to nose. "Look at me."

She opened her eyes. And saw an emotional volcano about to erupt inside the normally calm and controlled man she thought she knew.

He cared. He cared so much it was radiating off him like a nuclear meltdown. It melted the ice fortress she'd erected around her heart all those years ago.

"I'm not letting you run away this time, Davina." His voice was deep and dark. "You can try if you want, but I'm not going to let you get away."

"Drew, I…" Her protest died as he pulled out slowly, so slowly, then thrust back in hard and fast. He did it again and again, until he pushed her into another orgasm.

He followed and as she came down off the high, she realized what he'd been chanting in her ear.

I love you.

Over and over.

Holy shit. He blinked a couple of times to be sure he was where he thought he was, and it wasn't all a dream. Balls deep inside Davina, her arms around him and her breasts pillowing his chest.

Her breath shook as she exhaled, her face glowing, her expression shifting from awe to surprise. He leaned down and set his lips against hers gently, giving her room and opportunity to turn away if she wanted. He kept the kiss soft, a tease and a taste of what they'd just done— were still doing.

He sucked on her bottom lip, nipped its ripe flesh

and soothed it with his tongue. He pulled back a fraction and she followed, chasing him.

He took over, igniting the kiss into something explosive, shifting so he could pet her breasts the way he knew she liked, making her moan and hook one leg over his.

Just like that he was hard again.

He began moving in her, slowly, savoring every moment of every stroke, wallowing in the swell of pleasure that rose as he picked up the pace and strength of his thrusts.

He'd missed this, *missed her.* The smell of her hair, the satin of her skin, and the music of her sighs and moans as he gave her every bit of himself.

They both came again. This time, when he kissed her slow and easy, he shifted to his side, taking her with him, holding her close.

She clutched at him and he reveled in her acceptance. Until he realized she was crying.

"Davina? What's wrong?" He hadn't held back, given her all he had. "Shit, did I hurt you?"

His questions seemed to make her cry harder.

"Davina? Talk to me. Please."

She shook her head and held on to him like he was her anchor.

Uncertain as to the cause, and unwilling to let her go while she was this upset, he held her close, using his body to warm her, his hands stroking her back.

Finally, after several minutes, she calmed and pushed against his chest.

He loosened his hold, but only so far. She was going to talk if he had to make love to her a hundred times.

"It never made sense," she mumbled.

"What never made sense?" he asked, tilting her head up so he could see her expression.

"You and me."

"Bullshit."

She gave him a hollow-sounding laugh. "No, really. You're the hottest guy I've ever seen, smart, too, and you wanted me? A geeky girl who likes puzzles, popcorn, and prefers working with the dead. We're not even in the same league."

"You're the one out of my league," he said, kissing her softly. "I'm just a washed-up football player. You're a doctor with more brains than any one person should have and top it all off, you look like a wet dream come to life."

"I do not."

"Do so."

"My nose is too big and my lips are, well, too big, too."

"Your nose is perfect and your lips…" He was hard again just thinking about her lips. "I fantasize about having them around my cock." He thrust one leg between hers and turned them so he was on top again. "Your breasts make my mouth water. Especially since I can make you come just from sucking your nipples."

She stared up at him, her mouth open slightly, her eyes wide. A tear spilled out and trickled down to her ear. "But you'll leave me."

"No," he said, kissing her with all the gentleness he had. "Never. I have *never* stopped loving you."

"How can I believe you? It nearly killed me the last time. I…I loved you so much."

"I swear to you, there's no one else for me. You're my one."

She started to cry again.

"What can I do to convince you?"

Tears flooded her eyes and trailed down her face. "I don't know."

Fuck, she wasn't listening. The second he let her off the

bed she was going to retreat, mentally and physically.

"Will you give me a chance to prove it to you? Please?" He kissed her and kissed her. "I only want you."

She calmed finally, and wiped her face. "Okay, but I don't know—"

"I don't know, either," he interrupted. "But I'm going to figure this out." He brought his face down to hers until they were nose to nose. "I will."

He let her up so she could shower and while she was out of sight and earshot for a few minutes, he made a couple of calls.

The hotel restaurant was crowded—every table occupied and people waiting for tables to become available—but when she and Drew arrived, the hostess seated them at a table for two in the center of the room.

It seemed like everyone was watching them.

Davina shook her head at her own paranoia and focused on reading the menu. When the waitress came to take their drink order, Drew ordered her favorite red wine, then smiled at her so wide, she knew—*knew*—he was planning something crazy.

Did she want crazy?

She closed her menu then folded her hands in her lap to keep them from shaking. Ever since they'd made love, *twice*, that morning, she'd felt unbalanced. Uncertain. Unsure of what she wanted.

Her breathing grew shallow as all of those unwanted feelings tangled up her lungs.

And now she was going to cry again.

"Hey, gorgeous," Drew said, reaching around the table to take one of her hands in his. "You okay?"

She shook her head, just a little shake, but it was

enough to make her want to run away.

"Hmm. I was going to do this later, but maybe I need to do it now." He seemed oddly hesitant.

She met his gaze. "Do what?"

He smiled at her, and keeping hold of her hand, got out of his chair and went to one knee in front of her. His free hand went into a pocket and came out with a small jeweler's box. "I've had this since my grandmother passed away." He flicked it open to reveal a diamond ring. "Will you marry me?"

She stared at the ring, shock having frozen her breathing entirely. "What?"

"I've lived too many years already without you."

She looked into his face and found an open vulnerability there she'd never seen before.

That's when she realized the whole restaurant had gone silent. No voices talking or cutlery clanking as people ate. She glanced around.

Everyone was watching the two of them. Most were smiling, but a few, notably women, weren't.

She looked at Drew again and sucked in a breath. "You…promise?"

His smile lit up the room. "Yes. Do you?"

God, she wanted him. Not just for now, but for always. "Yes."

She was in his arms and the room erupted in cheers and shouts of congratulations.

"So," he asked in a whisper that was hers alone "your room or mine?"

She snorted a laugh. "Mine."

About…

Julie Rowe's first career as a medical lab technologist in Canada took her to the North West Territories and northern Alberta, where she still resides. She loves to include medical details in her romance novels, but admits she'll never be able to write about all her medical experiences because, "No one would believe them!" In addition to writing contemporary and historical medical romance, and fun romantic suspense for Entangled Publishing and Carina Press, Julie has short stories in Fool's Gold, the Mammoth Book of ER Romance, Timeless Keepsakes and Timeless Escapes anthologies. Her book SAVING THE RIFLEMAN (book #1 WAR GIRLS) won the novella category of the 2013 Gayle Wilson Award of Excellence. AIDING THE ENEMY (book #3 WAR GIRLS) won the novella category of the 2014 Colorado Romance Writer's Award of Excellence. Her writing has also appeared in several magazines such as Romantic Times Magazine, Today's Parent, and Canadian Living.

♥♥♥

For more information about Julie, please visit her online at www.julieroweauthor.com, on Twitter @julieroweauthor, or at her Facebook page: www.facebook.com/JulieRoweAuthor.

Interested in reading more medical romance and adventure? Julie's newest series The Biological Response Team begins with *Deadly Strain*, releasing June 15, 2015.

A sniper tries to protect an infectious disease specialist while they combat a deadly new bacterial strain, but he might not be able to stop her from making the ultimate sacrifice in order to save him. www.julieroweauthor.com

♥♥♥

Check out Julie's published backlist of books! www.julieroweauthor.com

♥♥♥

"The way these two characters played off of each other was absolutely brilliant." Review of *Hollywood Scandal* from Bitten by Romance

"…The Fast and the Furious meets Beauty and the Beast" review of *Molly Gets Her Man* from @BookswBenefits

♥♥♥

Julie's War Girls series is set in German-occupied Belgium during World War One. Discover danger, daring, and passion with three nurses who risk their lives to save the men they call their own.

Saving the Rifleman - John and Maria's story.
Enticing the Spymaster - Michael and Jude's story.
Aiding the Enemy - Herman and Rose's story.

♥♥♥

For contemporary stories of adventure and romance set at the top and the bottom of the world, look for *Icebound* and *North of Heartbreak* at your favorite ebook retailer.

Enjoy more Timeless Tales by

Ruth A. Casie ~ Lita Harris ~ Emma Kaye ~
Nicole S. Patrick ~ Julie Rowe

♥♥♥

Available Now

Timeless Keepsakes
A Collection of Christmas Stories

*Join us on five remarkable journeys that heal old wounds, remind us
of days gone by, play matchmaker, sweep us back in time and prove
that love can conquer all.*

Timeless Escapes
A Collection of Summer Stories

*Escape to the Virgin Islands where the bonds of marriage are
renewed, friends become lovers, and new love is given a chance to
thrive.*

Timeless Treasures
Stories of the Heart

*A special wish of hope, strength, and love brings five couples what
they treasure most in this heartwarming collection of short stories.*

♥♥♥

To receive up-to-date information on future
Timeless Scribes publications, visit our website at
www.TimelessScribes.com and sign up for our
mailing list.

Timeless Scribes
Publishing